keeper

illustrations by august hall

kathi appelt

keeper

Atheneum Books for Young Readers

NEW YORK   LONDON   TORONTO   SYDNEY

For Rose and TA, Merfolk

ATHENEUM BOOKS FOR YOUNG READERS

An imprint of Simon & Schuster Children's Publishing Division

1230 Avenue of the Americas, New York, New York 10020

This book is a work of fiction. Any references to historical events, real people, or real locales are used fictitiously. Other names, characters, places, and incidents are products of the author's imagination, and any resemblance to actual events or locales or persons, living or dead, is entirely coincidental.

Text copyright © 2010 by Kathi Appelt

Illustrations copyright © 2010 by August Hall

ATHENEUM BOOKS FOR YOUNG READERS is a registered trademark of Simon & Schuster, Inc.

For information about special discounts for bulk purchases, please contact Simon & Schuster Special Sales at 1-866-506-1949 or business@simonandschuster.com.

The Simon & Schuster Speakers Bureau can bring authors to your live event. For more information or to book an event, contact the Simon & Schuster Speakers Bureau at 1-866-248-3049 or visit our website at www.simonspeakers.com.

Book design by Debra Sfetsios

The text for this book is set in Centaur MT.

The illustrations for this book are rendered in mixed media.

Manufactured in the United States of America

0310 MTN

First Edition

10 9 8 7 6 5 4 3 2 1

CIP data for this book is available from the Library of Congress.

ISBN 978-1-4169-5060-8

alled out to her.

turned this whole day into a

s!

pe that held her boat to the

t to untie it. She needed the

uld make the tide rise, then

uld make the rope go slack,

could untie the knot, which

et her plan into action. Her

implored. Didn't it know

soon as she said the word

r bottom lip. So much had

moon, a blue moon, second

song.

night-blooming cyrus.

d depended upon the blue

one, had been ruined.

"I have heard the mermaids singing, each to each,
I do not think that they will sing for me."

—T.S. Eliot,

"The Love Song of J. Alfred Prufrock"

all ten of them had
Those ten crabs ha
disaster.

Stupid, stupid, stupid cra
Keeper checked the r
pier. It was still too tig
moon to rise, which wo
the boat rise, which wo
which would mean she
would mean she could s
perfect plan.

"Come on, moon," sh
she was in a hurry? As
"moon," she chewed on h
depended upon tonight's
full moon of the month.
First, Signe's gumbo.
Then, Dogie's two-word
Finally, Mr. Beauchamp's
All three of those things h
moon, and all of them, ever

Ruined by . . . CRABS!

Keeper never wanted to see another crab in her entire life! Never, never, never!

And now she needed the moon to turn the tide around and pull her out of the pond, through the channel, and into the breakers until she got to the sandbar.

That was the plan . . . or at least the first part of the plan.

2

What makes a ten-year-old girl think she can go out in a boat alone, at night, with only her dog for a sailing mate?

Well . . . muscles. Exactly!

Sitting in *The Scamper*, curling her arms up like a boxer, Keeper flexed her muscles. She certainly was not like the Incredible Hulk, but she was proud of her strong arms.

Recently, Dogie, her next-door neighbor and the proprietor of Dogie's Beach Umbrella and Surfboard Shop, which had at one time been a yellow school bus but was now simply known as "the Bus," had put her in charge of waxing the surfboards. It was a job she took seriously. Dogie called her his "wax-wing," which Keeper knew was some sort of bird because Dogie loved birds. He was always drawing them for one thing. Lots of pictures of birds. And even though waxing surfboards had nothing to do with birds at all, she still loved being called his waxwing.

He didn't pay her much—a cold Dr Pepper, plus one dollar for waxing a short board or two for waxing a long board—but she was proud of her work. She kept her dollars in an old red purse in her closet, a purse that Signe had picked up for her at the Tater Thrift Shop for fifty cents. To date, Keeper had $42.00 in that purse. She did not know what she was going to spend it on, but she liked knowing it was there, adding up.

And then one day Signe came home from work and handed her a copy of a Sears catalogue, the "Wish Book" edition. The only time Keeper had opened it, she randomly turned to a page with men's corduroy jackets and decided that there wasn't anything in that wish book that she wished to have, especially a man's corduroy jacket.

"Save it," Signe told her. "You might need it for a rainy day." So Keeper did.

Each time Dogie paid her to wax a surfboard, she put the money in her red purse, and then she put the purse on the shelf in her closet. The catalogue gathered dust.

3

The job of waxing is more complicated than it sounds.

Step 1: Keeper had to wash the salt water off of the board. Because there was no running water at the Bus, Dogie had attached a string of water hoses from his house all the way down the road to the Bus. This meant that Keeper had to run back and forth from house to Bus to turn the water on and off. It wasn't that far, maybe fifty yards, but she had to hurry anyway. "N-n-no n-n-need to waste water," Dogie always told her.

Step 2: She had to remove the old wax. First she had to scrape the whole deck of the board with a thing called a "comb," which looked a little like a hair comb, but instead of long, thin teeth, it had small, squatty teeth, perfect for jabbing underneath the old wax. This was the hardest part, especially when the wax was majorly caked on and gunky. Keeper had to press down on the comb with both hands to pry the old wax off.

It wasn't such a bad job when she was working on one of the short boards—five feet or so. But the long boards were a pain. Imagine eight to ten feet of gunked-up wax, and there you have it.

The wax went everywhere. It got underneath her fingernails, it stuck to her clothes, it clumped up on the top of her shoes. *Blech!*

Dogie had one old surfboard called a "gun" that was almost eleven feet long. Keeper hated waxing the gun, with its pointed ends. According to Dogie, wannabe surfers used it to "g-g-gun for the b-b-big waves." Thank goodness for Keeper, it didn't get rented too often. Even though she liked getting two dollars instead of one, the gun took F-O-R-E-V-E-R.

After she got the bulk of the old wax off, she finished removing the rest by rubbing the entire board with a product called Pickle Wax Remover. The

Pickle was squishy in her hand and felt like a beanbag, only instead of being stuffed with beans, it was filled with a powdery substance that felt softer than silk. Keeper didn't know what was in it, only that it got the old wax off. It also made the skin on her fingertips all pruny, like raisins. After she wiped all of the wax off, Keeper stood back and admired the shiny, clean board.

Dogie's surfboards were like works of art. Splashed across their rainbow-colored decks were air-brushed paintings of waterfalls and sea dragons and a host of other fantastic creatures. Her favorite painting was a winged horse that looked like part horse and part comet, with its long tail blazing down the length of the board.

Dogie had told her that a good ride in the surf was "l-l-like f-f-flying." Keeper wouldn't know since she had never ever been on a surfboard. "Wh-wh-when you're older," Dogie promised.

That promise was small consolation because Keeper thought that anyone old enough to *wax* a surfboard should be old enough to *ride* one, but in this matter of unfairness Signe had put her foot down. "No way, missy," Signe had told her, time after time. "I've already pulled you out of the surf twice, and that's enough."

Whenever Keeper appealed this decision to Dogie, he just shrugged.

Step 2a: Once Keeper removed the wax, she checked the board for any dings, cuts, or notches in the fiberglass skin, so that Dogie could repair it with a ding repair kit. This was a critical responsibility. If a ding went unrepaired, the board would take on water and make it heavier than it should be. Then it wouldn't be as easy to maneuver.

"A w-w-waxwing has to f-f-find d-d-dings," Dogie told her. So she did. Surfers put dings in the boards all the time. Especially if they accidentally ran up on the sandbar. Dogie was constantly warning them about that sandbar. De Vaca's Rock.

Step 3: This was when Keeper applied the new wax, beginning with the base coat. Keeper knew this was an important step too. If the base coat wasn't applied just so, then the whole wax job could be a big, fat mess, and then she'd have to start over. The key to *Step 3*, according to Dogie, was waxing in the right direction: "N-n-nose to t-t-tail, rail t-t-to rail," he told her, which meant "start at the top and work your way to the bottom by going side to side." So Keeper pressed the bar of base coat wax on its edge, then in small, precise circles she covered the entire deck of the board with an undercoating of sticky, bumpy wax. In fact, her favorite brand of wax was called Sticky Bumps. True to its name, it made the smooth deck all sticky and bumpy.

"S-s-so the s-s-surfer will st-st-stick," said Dogie. If the wax was too smooth, the surfer wouldn't be able to grip the board with his or her toes. Wipe out!

Step 4: Last step. The wax itself. The kind of wax Keeper used for this step depended upon the water temperature. Most of the time the water temperature of the Gulf of Mexico hovered in the 70s or 80s; only in the winter months did it drop into the

60s and upper 50s. Because Keeper had been Dogie's waxwing only since late spring, and it was still summer, she used Sticky Bumps Day Glo wax for warmer water. The hot pink of it seemed to scream at her while she rubbed it on top of the base coat. When it turned cooler in the coming fall and winter months, she thought she would switch to the Tour Series, which smelled faintly of bananas.

Dogie had a package of it waiting for her in the Bus.

All that scraping and waxing, all that nose-to-tail, rail-to-rail, Day-Glo-banana-scented action, gave a girl muscles.

She would need those muscles tonight for steering the boat.

4

Keeper dipped her fingers into the water beside the boat and stirred it in a quick circle. Right then, in the dark, deep night, the pond was as still as glass. "Hurry up, tide," she muttered.

Then she added, "Stupid, stupid crabs!"

The water was cool compared to the warm night air. She knew those ten crabs were down there. That very morning she had watched them, one by one, scurry into the water. A parade of crabs.

Suddenly, an image of their clacking claws made her yank her hand out of the pond. She stuck it, wet, into her shorts pocket and bumped her fingertips against the small wooden carving of Yemaya. Keeper had jammed the figurine into her pocket on her way out of her bedroom, right before she sneaked out of

the house. Yemaya, queen of the sea, head mermaid. She was one of seven, carved for Keeper by Mr. Beauchamp. She called them the "merlings."

"Yemaya," Keeper whispered. She rubbed the figurine—it was one of her favorites. Across from her in the boat, her dog, BD, whined. She reached over to give him a rub too.

All at once, a small gust of wind bumped against her; a reminder. It wasn't just the crabs that had caused all of this trouble. She had to admit that the crabs had company: Sinbad (cat) and Too (dog) and Captain (seagull) and BD (dog). The "beasts," as Dogie called them. Those four were party to the mayhem too.

"Why, yes," she said to BD, as if the dog were protesting, "you most certainly were." But then another little gust blew by.

The beasts weren't the only ones at fault, no-siree-bob. Keeper knew—she herself was also, at least partially, probably, a little, a tiny bit, more than that, well, okay, yes, she was also to blame.

"Stupid!" she said.

She leaned over the boat's edge again and made the maddest, angriest face she could think of and hoped that the crabs could see it. But it was so dark, she couldn't even see her own reflection.

Which was just as well. She had seen enough mad faces in the past day. She glared straight up at the black sky. Sugary stars blinked back at her. "Where are you, poky ol' moon?" she asked. "Hurry up!"

Keeper knew that a full moon should rise soon after the sun had set, and it seemed like the sun had set forever ago. But then she thought about what Mr. Beauchamp told her: "Blue moon might hide behind a cloud bank, might dillydally behind sand dunes. Blue moon . . . takes her time."

5

The day had not started out with mad faces. It had actually started out with glad faces. Keeper had only barely been awake that morning when she had walked into the kitchen at the same time that Dogie walked through their screen door holding his large aluminum tub. Keeper knew it was filled with snapping crabs. Signe was already stirring the thick roux that would make the base for her gumbo. Keeper walked over to the tub to make the crab count. Suddenly, a small shiver ran along her arms.

"Hey, s-s-sleepyhead," said Dogie. He winked at her.

"Hey, yourself," Keeper said, whereupon she forgot about the shiver and winked back. This day had finally arrived! Which meant that the night she had been waiting for all summer would be along in only hours. Blue moon night! Blue moon gumbo! Mr. Beauchamp's blooming flowers! And one more thing. The one more thing that made her face the gladdest: Dogie's two-word song, the one that he would finally sing for Signe that very night, the one he had practiced all summer with his ukulele: *"Marry me!"*

Keeper had listened to him sing it while she waxed the surfboards and Signe wasn't around. *"Marry me!"* Dogie had sung it over and over, with not one single stutter.

That morning Keeper wondered, *Would Signe say yes?* That was a question for the universe, but Keeper hoped so. Oh yes, she hoped so.

Then Dogie would be even more like a real-life father, wouldn't he? Keeper almost blurted it all out, right then, but instead, she put her hands over her mouth. It took every single cell in her body to keep from squealing. She smiled a majorly happy smile at him and crossed her fingers.

Keeper had known Dogie since the moment she was born, born in the water.

"L-l-like a d-d-dolphin," he had told her. Too, Dogie's little pup, stood on his hind legs and did his own funny dance. Keeper reached down and scratched his spotted head.

"G-g-got a c-c-couple of b-b-boards need waxing," Dogie told her. Keeper kept smiling. That meant at least two more dollars for her red purse. By the end of the day she would have $44.00. A fortune! What a lucky day! Now she watched Dogie scoop up little Too and open the door. "G-g-gotta go," he said. Then she looked over at Signe and saw her turn her face away from the steaming roux and smile at him.

"Adios," Signe said, adding some sort of spice or another to the pot.

Keeper watched Dogie cast his eyes at Signe as he stepped onto the porch. "B-b-blue moon t-t-tonight," he said as he closed the door.

Keeper wanted to rush out behind him and beg him to sing his song now; she wasn't sure she could wait all the livelong day.

She listened to his heavy footsteps going down the

wooden stairs. She counted. *Ten, nine, eight, seven, six, five, four, three, two* . . . He paused. There were ten steps between the porch and the ground. Would he come back up? Maybe he couldn't wait the livelong day either!

Keeper bit her tongue.

One.

There it was, the last step. Shoot. Dogie was gone. But her glad face was still there.

6

Keeper was still smiling when she walked to the stove and stood next to Signe, who was stirring the bubbling liquid for her blue moon gumbo. The smell filled the room. Keeper thought that if she held out her tongue in the steamy kitchen, she'd be able to taste the spicy mixture without even putting a spoonful in her mouth.

Onions, garlic, bacon, all stirred together with a mysterious spice called *"filé."*

"It's made from sassafras leaves," Signe told her as she chopped up the okra and tomatoes, brought home fresh from the Tater Grocery & Market the day before.

Keeper *loved loved loved* that smell. "It smells scrumptious," she told Signe. The spicy scent settled on her skin.

Keeper knew that the pot would sit on the stove top all day, simmering and stewing, and at the last minute, just before she served it, Signe would drop the crabs into a pot of boiling water, one at a time, and then add them to the gumbo.

Fresh crabs.

Caught in Dogie's net just hours ago.

Blue crabs.

Tasty crabs.

In that very moment Keeper became intensely aware of the crabs in the tub. She could hear their pinchers snapping in a nervous frenzy. But when she squatted down next to them, they stopped and became perfectly still. For the first time ever, she noticed the delicate markings on their shells, saw the perfect symmetry of their heart-shaped backs and the imperfect balance of their large and small claws. Suddenly, the crabs seemed beautiful to her, all of them facing her, looking up at her.

Oh no! she thought. Signe was going to drop them into boiling water, drop them in alive. Their wonderful shells, blue and brown and white, would turn pink and then red in the hot liquid. Keeper's stomach did a flip. She couldn't look at them.

She turned away from the tub and hurried to the bathroom, where she sat down hard on the edge of the bathtub. The porcelain finish felt ice cold through the seat of her pajamas. Her heart beat like mad against her chest. As mad as the crabs. She grabbed one of her great-grandmother's white cotton towels and bit it.

What to do?

She didn't think she had ever been "looked at" by a tubful of crabs. Goose bumps ran down her back. Were they trying to tell her something?

Next she heard Signe knock at the door. "Keeper, honey?"

She should say something. But what?

"Keeper?"

In the bathroom she could not hear the crabs. Thank goodness. Her heart slowed down. She took a deep breath, then rose to open the door. Then she stopped. How had she not thought of it before? That the crabs were boiled alive? Suddenly she realized that the crabs were sending her a message: *Help us!* And that message was coming through loud and clear.

And how did the crabs know what dire fate awaited them? But if they didn't know, why would they call out to her? And they had called out to her. She was certain of it. She draped the towel over her head and held the edges under her chin.

She had never felt any affinity for crabs. Plenty of times she had been nipped on the side of the foot or on the toe by one as she walked through the shallow waves on the beach. But they had never looked at her before either. Also, she never fully realized how lovely their shells were. She sat back down on the edge of the tub. She couldn't bear the thought of them being dropped into the boiling water. She heard the knock on the door. She didn't know what to do. She didn't want to hear the crabs. But it wouldn't be good for Signe to think that she was sick. That would mean a whole day of staying in bed.

There was nothing worse than staying in bed on a summer day. And not only that, but she was supposed to go to the Bus to wax the two surfboards, plus she needed to help Mr. Beauchamp water his plants. And what if Signe made her miss the two-word song? The one that Dogie was supposed to sing that very night? She heard the knock again. She had to open the door. But if she did, she'd hear the crabs.

Open?

Not open.

Knock, knock, knock.

"Keeper?"

Stay in bed on a summer day? Maybe miss Dogie's song? Miss hearing Signe's response? No!

No-no-no-no-no!

"Okay, okay," she said. She stood up and leaned against the door. On the other side she knew that Signe was standing there with her wooden spoon in one hand. Signe's bright white hair stood up in spikes. Keeper loved Signe's hair. According to Signe, her hair turned white when she was only fourteen, right before she left Iowa. It had been snow white ever since. At once Keeper realized that she had never asked Signe what color her hair had been before it turned white. Had it been black like hers? Auburn like Dogie's?

Purple?

Pink?

Green? Mr. Beauchamp, their elderly neighbor across the road, had told her that the Russian mermaids, the *rusalki*, had green hair.

Hair.

It came in so many colors.

Like red.

Red like boiled crabs.

Boiled crabs.

Boiled alive.

There was the message again. Keeper couldn't deny it. She knew what she had heard, even though she really hadn't heard it, had she? Technically, all she heard were snipping-snapping claws, but the message was coming through nonetheless. She started to pant. She tugged on the towel. The message zoomed around her head, buzzed in her ears.

"Are you all right?" Signe asked from the other side of the door.

Was she all right? She wasn't sure.

Keeper shook her head. "I'm okay," she said. But was she? She was standing in the bathroom with a towel over her head, and she was sure she had just gotten a message from a tubful of blue crabs.

Was this what it was like to have mermaid blood running through your veins?

7

Now, hours later, Keeper sat in the boat with BD.

Of the four people who lived along Oyster Ridge Road, Keeper was the only one who was not a grown-up. "I'm the only one with merblood, too," she told BD as they sat in the small boat, the darkness as thick as stew.

The boat rocked. She had tried to discuss this fact with Signe before, only to have Signe cross her arms and say, "Keeper, let's be practical here," and then change the subject to homework or feeding BD or washing the dishes.

Now Signe was furious with her, and Signe wasn't the only one. So were Mr. Beauchamp and Dogie.

E-V-E-R-Y-O-N-E.

Signe called the terrain of Oyster Ridge Road the "world unto itself."

Here's a fact: Everyone in the world unto itself was mad at Keeper.

"There's only one person who can help us, BD," she told the dog. "My mother."

Then she added, "The mermaid."

As she sat there, atop the glassy pond, Keeper solemnly put her left hand on her chest, just below the charm that hung from her neck. There she felt her heartbeat under the skin of her palm. The charm was icy cold. She could feel the cold of it even through her T-shirt. Then, with her right hand, she patted her pocket where the carving of Yemaya sat. She could feel the small outlines of the figurine against the denim of her shorts.

"For luck, BD," she said. Between the charm and the figurine, she figured she was loaded with luck. "Good luck," she told the dog. Then she followed with, "We've had enough of that other kind."

8

At the sound of his name, BD thumped his tail against the bottom of the boat. BD, short for Best Dog. He felt Keeper rub the soft fur behind his ears. In return, he gave her a slurpy kiss.

"Ugh . . . stealth kiss!" Keeper complained, then he watched her wipe her chin with the back of her hand.

BD whined. *Please, can we go back now? Please?* For emphasis, he put his right front paw on her knee. *Please, please, please,* he whined.

He was worried about Keeper. He could tell she wasn't happy.

He was worried about the dark. He did not like the dark.

He was worried about being in the boat this late at night when they should be sound asleep in Keeper's room just down the hall from Signe's room.

Worry. It was worse than sand fleas. Suddenly he itched all over.

Keeper patted his paw atop her knee. "It's okay, boy," she said. Then she added, "You'll see. It'll be easy peasy."

The dog licked her chin again. He didn't think being in this boat in the middle of the night was easy at all.

"After all," she told him, "you're the finder dog." That was true. Over the years BD had found a whole host of missing objects—the odd sock, a misplaced spoon, the tiny key to the lock on Keeper's diary, one of Signe's peace-sign earrings, loose pages of homework.

He also found other things, things that weren't missing until he found them, like one-of-a-kind seashells and tiny abandoned puppies, including Too, who was adopted by Dogie. He even found shooting stars and stripey geckos, things that came and went. But right now BD wasn't so much a finder dog as a worry dog.

9

Keeper leaned over the boat's side again. "I know you're down there," she said to the black water. She cupped her hands over her ears. Would the crabs call to her again? She hoped not. She did not ever want to hear anything at all from crabs, never ever, not in a million bajillion years, not one single crabby peep.

"Stupid crabs!"

How, she wondered, could ten stupid crabs cause so much trouble?

T-R-O-U-B-L-E.

She rested her chin on the side of the boat and peered into the water. She could hear Signe's words in her brain: *"You're in trouble, missy."*

"All because of you stupid crabs," muttered Keeper to the water.

If only she had stayed in the bathroom that morning, with the towel over her head. Why hadn't she? If she had stayed in the bathroom all day, none of this would have happened. She would not have heard the crabs at all, because by the time she came out, Signe would have boiled them and added them to the gumbo.

But . . . she hadn't stayed in the bathroom, had she? Nope. After all, how could Keeper stay in the bathroom all day long? Was the bathroom a good place for a girl to spend the day? Was it a comfortable place to pass the hours? A fun place to hang out on a summer day? Was there anything at all interesting about the bathroom? No. No. And double no.

So instead of staying there, Keeper had followed Signe back to the kitchen. Didn't Signe hear the crabs also? Keeper didn't think so. She didn't think that Signe had any merblood in her. In fact, she *knew* that Signe didn't have any merblood. Signe, after all, was not her real mother.

That would be Meggie Marie.

All at once, watching Signe stir the gumbo, Keeper

got another message, this one from the universe: *Set those crabs free.* The thought immediately made her feel hugely better. Freeing the crabs was the answer.

But the answer led to a question: How could she carry that gigantic tub of screaming crabs past Signe, out the door and down the steps, and then all the way to the beach, which was at least a hundred yards from the house?

She didn't think she could.

Could she? Hmmm . . . Wait!

Of course!

The answer was so simple: just ask!

Exactly.

So Keeper asked, "Do we *have* to put the crabs in the gumbo?"

Signe turned around, spoon in the air. "What?" Keeper noticed that when she asked the question, the crabs stopped scuttling.

"The crabs," repeated Keeper. "Do we have to put them in the gumbo?"

"Keeper, it's *crab* gumbo."

"I know . . . but just this once, could we have . . . sausage gumbo?" She smiled her nicest, most very nice smile at Signe. "Everyone would be happy with sausage."

"Don't be silly," said Signe. "Anyway, you love crab gumbo."

Keeper knew that was true . . . once . . . she *used* to love crab gumbo. She did not want to say it out loud in front of the crabs, who were now completely silent. Were they reaching a state of resignation? Did they understand that they were doomed? She glanced at them. If it were possible for crabs to look resigned, these crabs did. Keeper couldn't stand it.

"Besides," Signe's voice interrupted her contemplation, "if we don't use the crabs, we might hurt Dogie's feelings." Then she added, "After all, he got up at dawn this morning to catch them."

Keeper had forgotten about Dogie. The last thing she ever wanted to do was hurt Dogie's feelings.

The crabs shuffled around a little. Keeper sighed.

Just yesterday, Mr. Beauchamp had told her, "All the stars are lining up." Keeper knew that that meant that something significant was about to happen, and she knew that the gumbo was an important ingredient.

Gumbo. Ukulele. Night-blooming cyrus.

Stars in a line.

All on a blue moon night.

She watched Signe lift the cutting board and scrape a mound of chopped green peppers into the pot. "Plus," said Signe, "we always have crab gumbo on the blue moon. It's our family tradition."

Keeper put her elbows on the table and rested her head on her hands. The steam from the pot settled on her arms. She felt clammy all over.

Suddenly, as if to remind her of their plight, the crabs began to raise a ruckus again. She tried not to look at them. But she couldn't help it.

One. Two. Three. Four. Five. Six. Seven. Eight. Nine. Ten.

She didn't even notice BD until he rubbed his wet nose against her leg. It was so cold, it made her bare toes curl. She patted the dog. Did he feel bad for the crabs too?

Then, out of the blue, Keeper caught a lucky break.

"Oh no," said Signe. She held a small empty jar in the air. "How could this happen?" Signe shook the empty jar, as if by shaking it, she could make the missing ingredient somehow appear.

"What is it?" asked Keeper.

"Pepper sauce," said Signe. "I don't have any pepper sauce!"

"Does it matter?" asked Keeper.

"Petite Tartine Red Pepper Sauce," replied Signe. "I need it." Then she pointed to the recipe in the old cookbook and stated, "Finest pepper sauce in the country."

Keeper knew it was the only pepper sauce that Signe ever used, and she only used it in gumbo. Now she was out. The jar was empty.

The pot bubbled on the burner. Signe turned down the flame so that it would simmer, and then she scratched her forehead. Then, to Keeper's great surprise, she asked, "Keeper, can you keep an eye on this while I run to town?"

Keeper couldn't believe her ears. For the last several weeks she had been working hard to prove that she was responsible enough to stay home alone, at least for short periods.

She had taken care of all her chores without being asked (twice) . . . she had kept her clothes up off the floor . . . she had washed the dog every week. And also, after all, didn't she have her own job at the Bus? Wasn't she the official waxwing? Hadn't she made $42.00? And wasn't she going to make at least $2.00 more that very day?

Wasn't all of that "responsible"?

Usually, no matter how small the errand, Signe made Keeper ride along with her. Either that, or she made her stay with Mr. Beauchamp, or she sent her down to Dogie's Bus to wait for her. In fact, the Bus or Mr. Beauchamp's place was where she went while Signe worked her shifts at the Prince Oyster Bar and

Bar. But today was not a workday for Signe. Today was a gumbo day.

Now with the empty pepper sauce jar in the air, a golden opportunity rose in front of Keeper.

"I'll only be gone for a few moments," said Signe. "I'll be right back." As Signe walked through the door, she turned around and added, "Keeper, if the gumbo starts to boil again, turn down the flame and stir it, or else we'll have gumbo everywhere."

Keeper nodded and waved, a small little wave. Her heart thumped inside her rib cage. She watched the door close.

Alone!

She was all by herself.

With the crabs.

She did a quick calculation.

A drive to Tater and back, added to a quick trip into the store. Thirty minutes. At the most, Signe would be gone thirty minutes.

At the most.

The ten crabs looked more beautiful than ever, their backs shaped like wide hearts.

Keeper pointed at BD. "We've got a job to do."

"Woof," he replied, "woof!" Then he ducked under the table and kept his distance.

Keeper felt a happy rush of gladness skitter down her legs and over her toes. But she had to hurry. Signe would be back in thirty minutes, not a minute more.

10

In the driveway Signe turned the key in the ignition of the Dodge station wagon. She waited a moment for the engine to warm up, and while it did, she said her customary blessing of gratitude that the old V8 had started.

It was in this very car, behind this same steering wheel, that Meggie Marie had driven onto the shoulder of the highway and picked Signe up all those years ago.

There Signe had stood, all alone on the side of the road, with only a large wooden bowl, her only possession in the world, held tightly against her chest, just a few dollar bills stuffed into her shoe, no luggage, no nothing, except a large wooden bowl and a huge desire to escape from the closed-in terrain of central Iowa.

This very same green Dodge station wagon had

swept Signe up and brought her here to this remote strip of beach along the Texas coast. No mile upon mile of cornfields here. No grain silos marching along the horizon. No wintry snow piled up in heaps. No rooms full of memories; memories of her parents, who had been killed in a car accident when she was only eleven.

Only sand and palm trees and water. In Iowa, Signe had felt as locked in as the landscape. But not here, not on Oyster Ridge Road, world unto itself.

From the moment that she rode up to the old house with Meggie Marie, Signe had felt at home.

Today, as she drove past the gate of the state park that bordered Oyster Ridge Road, still clutching the empty bottle of Petite Tartine Red Pepper Sauce in her hand, she glanced in the rearview mirror. In it, she saw the haint blue house and caught her breath.

"Am I crazy?!" she suddenly asked herself. "I just left Keeper alone!" She pressed the brakes. The wheels squealed in response, and the car fishtailed back and forth on the road. Signe pulled over. What was she thinking? She started to turn around . . . but then . . . then . . . she thought about Dogie.

Usually, it wouldn't matter if she didn't have any Petite Tartine Red Pepper Sauce. It wouldn't have made a bit of difference. But tonight she needed the gumbo to be perfect. She needed every single ingredient to be just right. The moon would not be blue again for months, and by then she might lose her courage altogether. She needed Petite Tartine Red Pepper Sauce.

She stepped on the gas pedal and drove toward town, at least ten miles an hour faster than she usually drove. Thirty minutes. She shouldn't be gone longer than thirty minutes. If she hurried, maybe she could make it in twenty or twenty-five. She knew the exact spot on the shelves where the jars of sauces stood at the Tater Grocery & Market. Thirty minutes.

Max.

That was all.

11

As soon as Keeper heard the door slam and the car drive off, she grabbed the handle of the tub. A fifteen-gallon tub, filled partway with water and crabs, is not light. Dogie had carried it in earlier like it weighed five pounds, but when Keeper tried to lift it, she could hardly get it to budge. Even with her brand-new muscles from her job as waxwing, the tub was way too heavy for her to lift.

She'd just have to get some of that water out of there. The crabs were quiet now, but she still felt them urging her on. "I'm hurrying," she told them. One of the bigger ones reached above the water and snipped at her. She stepped back and let go of the handles. The water sloshed, splashing over the rim and onto the kitchen floor. "Rats!" Keeper muttered.

Now she'd have to mop it up before Signe got back. She opened the cabinet and found a measuring cup to scoop out the water.

Then she paused. All ten crabs had their pinchers up in the air. She wasn't about to lower her hand down into those pinchers. What to do? What to do? She looked at the clock on the stove. She had not checked it when Signe left, but she guessed that at least five minutes had passed.

The crabs seemed to be clacking their pinchers in time to the advancing clock.

Keeper lifted one end of the tub again, but it was no use. It probably weighed as much as she did—maybe more, actually, if she thought about it—but there wasn't time to compare her weight to the weight of the tub, not with that clock tick-tocking away!

She heard the brew on the stove begin to boil. She dashed over and gave it a good stir. She tapped the spoon on the side of the pot and then set it on the counter. That's when she noticed the big bowl. Signe's wooden bowl.

Keeper called it the "spinning bowl" because Signe had told her, "When I was a little girl, my mother would put the bowl on the kitchen floor and then set me in it and spin me around and around and around." It had been Signe's mother's bowl, and Signe had brought it all the way from Iowa.

There was a song too, a spinning song:

Spin, my little spinneroo,
Spin around the room.
Spin again and spin some more
Spin around the moon.

Whenever Signe finished the spinning song, she always smiled. And then she'd rub the bowl with her hand.

Keeper could picture a miniature Signe sitting in it.

Such a large bowl.

Large enough for a little girl.

Large enough for a *crab* or two.

Bingo!

She lifted the bowl and set it on the floor next to

the tub. Then she crossed her fingers and chanted, "Let there be bacon, let there be bacon, let there be bacon." Dogie had shown her how to catch a crab from the pier; all she needed was a piece of string and some bacon. She had watched him do it. She could do it now.

She found the string in the drawer next to the knives and forks. Then she closed her eyes and pulled open the refrigerator door.

"Let there be bacon, let there be bacon, oh please, let there be bacon."

She opened her eyes.

Bacon!

There was bacon.

"Bingo bingo bingo!" she cried.

She peeled off a strip of it and tied it to the string. Then she lowered it into the tub, right in front of a waiting crab. Sure enough, the crab latched on. Slowly, slowly, slowly, she lifted it out of the tub and right into the wooden bowl. She could see that there was plenty of room in the bowl for at least one more crab.

She cut another piece of string from the roll and tied another morsel of bacon onto it. Crab Number Two climbed aboard. Now she had two crabs munching bits of bacon in Signe's wooden bowl. Should she try to fit a third in there? She lifted the bowl and decided to leave it at two. Quickly, she slipped out the door and down the ten porch steps. She had to hurry.

At the bottom of the steps she paused. If she ran all the way to the beach, it would take too long. Signe would be back before then. Plus, she still had eight more crabs to rescue. She turned around. She would take them to the Cut. It didn't have much water in it this early in the day because of the low tide, but it would have to do. After all, crabs didn't need much water.

Keeper ran across the yard and down to the pond. She was right, there wasn't a lot of water in it, but soon enough, the tide would rise and fill it. Until then, there was enough for ten angry crabs.

She tilted the bowl on its side in the grass and watched as Numbers One and Two scuttled out. She stood there as they disappeared beneath the water.

Dogie's boat, *The Scamper*, tied to the pier, bumped against the wooden railings like a welcoming committee for the crustacean crew.

"Woof, woof!"

From outside the house, she could hear BD bark in the kitchen. His voice reminded her that she still had eight crabs to go. She had to hurry.

Up the stairs she ran.

String.

Bacon.

Slowly, slowly, slowly.

Plop! Into the bowl.

String.

Bacon.

Slowly, slowly, slowly.

Plop! Into the bowl.

Then out the door, down the steps, across the yard, and down to the Cut. Hurry, hurry, hurry. Signe would be back any minute.

12

From his perch on Mr. Beauchamp's porch, the cat Sinbad watched the girl across the way. He saw her carry the large bowl back and forth to the edge of the pond and then release some crabs.

Crabs! Sinbad had no use for crabs. In fact, Sinbad had no use for anyone except Mr. Beauchamp. They had been together for years and years, too many to count. They had an understanding, he and the old sailor. Mr. Beauchamp tended the house, and Sinbad did as he pleased, which meant he prowled the beach, teased BD, hissed at the very annoying seagull that rode on BD's back. Sinbad came and went with the tides, always arriving in time for dinner and a good rub behind his ears.

But lately, Mr. Beauchamp had been sleeping more

and more, sleeping too much. It worried the cat, all this sleeping. As he watched the girl scurry to and fro with the bowl and the crabs, he wondered if he should go inside and wake Mr. Beauchamp up. He looked at the morning surrounding him. It was still early.

No, he would let Mr. Beauchamp sleep a little longer. Then Sinbad fluffed his fur and moved into a new sunbeam and let the warmth of it soak into his skin. There, next to the clay pot that held the night-blooming cyrus, its heavy buds just on the cusp of bursting open, the cat yawned and licked his paws. He blinked. Then he drifted off into an early nap. He needed all of his energy for taunting the dog.

His favorite pastime.

13

Each time Keeper repeated the crab rescue process—string, bacon, crab, and so on—she got a little quicker. And with each foray, *splish, splash,* more and more salty water sloshed onto the slippery floor. Three more times, she caught a pair of crabs, lowered them into Signe's bowl, and carried them down to the Cut.

And in between, she stopped to stir the roux that grew thicker and thicker in its pot on the stove. The house was full of its spicy aroma. Keeper paused for just a moment and took a deep breath, then lowered the spoon. Her crab rescue operation was working.

Keeper pulled her shoulders back. "We're almost done," she told BD.

"Woof," he barked.

After the last trip, with all ten crabs safely set free in

the shallow water of the pond, she stood by the bank. A wave of relief washed over her. She looked at the bottom of the bowl. There was only a tiny scrap of bacon stuck to it. She lifted it out and dropped it in the grass. She rubbed her fingers together; they were greasy from the bacon. The sides of the bowl were greasy too. She'd have to wash it before Signe returned.

For a brief moment she considered dipping it into the water of the pond, to rinse it off, but straightaway she thought, *What if it got away from me?*

That wouldn't be good. With those crabs in the water, she did not want to wade into the pond to retrieve the wooden bowl. No way, no how, no sirree!

She started back for the house, and when she did, she noticed Sinbad napping on the porch rail at Mr. Beauchamp's house. *This bowl would be a perfect boat for a cat,* she thought. She turned and looked back at the water. It would be a perfect boat for a little girl, too, wouldn't it?

All at once, a cloud passed overhead. She thought about Signe sitting on her mother's kitchen floor, spinning in the bowl. Spinning and spinning and spinning. A wave of dizziness spun over her.

She needed to get the bowl back to its spot on the table. She checked once more to make sure the crabs were still in the water and not, for some reason, following her. All she saw was the silvery water, the shallow waves blinking at her in the morning sun.

For one wonderful moment she felt a bit like what a hero might feel like, even if she was a hero to only the resident crab population.

That's when she heard the familiar *crunch-crunch-pop* of oyster shells beneath car tires, along with the unmistakable chugging of an automobile engine. She'd recognize that sound anywhere.

"Oh no!" said Keeper.

"Woof!" barked BD. Then he barked again, "Woof!"

"Run!" she called to him.

Keeper gripped the bowl as hard as she could and ran up the stairs. The roux bubbled.

Hurry, hurry, hurry.

The sound of the station wagon on the crushed oyster shells grew louder. She shifted the heavy bowl into one hand and pulled open the door.

The clock ticked.

The roux boiled.

The door slammed behind her.

Everything was fine except for the watery floor. As soon as she stepped inside the door, *whoosh!*

Keeper slid into the side of the cabinet and managed to grab the edge of the counter without falling. But as she slid, the bowl, Signe's beautiful bowl, the one Signe's mother had set her in and spun her around and around, that bowl, the one that Signe had carried with her all the way from Iowa, the one that Keeper had just used to rescue the crabs, flipped into the air and landed, hard, on the ceramic tiles of the kitchen floor.

Ccccrrrrraaaaaacccckkkk!

The splitting of wood sounded like a firecracker. And at that very moment, in that exact second, at the precise instant that the bowl hit the floor, Signe walked in, and just like that, Keeper felt the heat in the room skyrocket.

BD shot down the hall and underneath Keeper's bed.

Signe stood in the doorway, her white hair ablaze. Then, what did Keeper hear, all at the same time?

1. The hiss of the roux as it slid down the outside of the pot and met the flame of the burner.
2. The thump of the jar of Petite Tartine Red Pepper Sauce as it fell out of Signe's hand and onto the floor.
3. Signe's voice shouting, "KEEPER!" so loud that BD whined and pushed his head between his paws.

Keeper knew this last part without even seeing it because that's what BD always did when Signe yelled.

Only one word seemed reasonable: Retreat!

And that's what Keeper did. She raced after BD to her bedroom and shut the door.

14

Signe's heart pounded. What on earth had happened? The floor was sopping wet, the bowl—her one single thing of her mother's!—was cracked in two, the gumbo was burnt.

How could Keeper have wreaked so much havoc in such a short time? Thirty minutes. Half an hour. It wasn't that long. But it was long enough for the gumbo to boil over. Long enough for Keeper to break her wooden bowl.

Signe pulled the pot of roux from the flame and turned the stove off. Without even looking, she knew it was a blackened mess. She popped the lid on it to keep the smoke down. Then she bent over and picked up the pieces of the bowl. They were greasy. She sniffed at one. It smelled like bacon. She scratched her head. Why bacon? She set the pieces on the counter and stared at them. Bacon?

What was Keeper doing with bacon?

Then she looked down into the large aluminum tub. There was only water. Not a single crab. All at once, Signe knew what Keeper had done. She had set those crabs free using bacon and her bowl.

Signe sank into a kitchen chair and stared at Keeper's closed bedroom door. The air in the kitchen was smoky from the burnt roux.

What in heaven's name had come over her girl?

Then Signe's heart pounded harder.

How could she have left Keeper by herself? Keeper was barely ten, still a little girl, a little girl who believed in elves and fairies and angels. . . . And always, she believed her mother herself was a mermaid, and Signe had let her believe it. Keeper, Signe knew, believed in magic.

But what, Signe wondered, did magic have to do with crabs exactly? As if the ruined gumbo wondered too, a single drop slid down the outside of the pot and hissed.

15

Now, in the deep, deep night, Keeper patted her pocket, felt the outlines of the wooden carving of Yemaya through her denim shorts.

Yemaya. Who was she?

According to Mr. Beauchamp, she was the *grand-mère* of all the waters.

Yemaya, the big mama.

Queen mother of the merfolk.

Chieftess of the whales and sea snakes.

Doyenne of the rivers and lakes and streams and bayous.

Of all the merfolk, Keeper loved Yemaya best.

Goddess of the deep.

Yemaya.

If you gave her a gift, she might grant a wish.

16

Wishes. Before today, Keeper had made plenty of wishes, like wishes on falling stars and wishes on rainbows and wishes on wishbones, all kinds of small wishes, like for Hershey's Kisses with almonds and tie-dyed shoelaces. But now she needed a big wish, a giant wish.

It had been a whole day full of mad, mad, mad, all starting with those crabs. Everyone, *everyone* in the world unto itself, was mad at her. All that mad had rattled the windowpanes, settled in the corners, rustled the curtains, made her skin feel sticky.

As the evening rolled in, the only thing Keeper could think to do was hunker down in her bedroom with a plate of cheddar cheese bites and sliced tomatoes for dinner. It was a sorry replacement for the spicy gumbo, but Keeper knew not to complain.

For hours the mad had swirled around in her bedroom air, chilly. Despite the warmth of the summer breeze drifting through her open window, Keeper's feet felt like Popsicles. She opened her top dresser drawer to find a pair of socks, and that's when she saw . . . the charm.

Her mother's charm!

The charm was the last thing her mother had given her before she swam away when Keeper was three, seven years ago. For seven years Keeper had kept it in her top dresser drawer. Right beneath her socks. Seven years.

Seven.

A lucky number!

"Yes!" Keeper had said as she lifted the charm out of the drawer. She had flopped down on the floor, lifted the bedskirt, and thrust it into BD's face. "Look!" she said. BD touched the charm with his nose, then pulled back. The charm was freezing cold, colder than Keeper's feet.

"Seven years," she told BD. "That's lucky."

Suddenly, her thoughts were racing. The charm had been given to her by her mother, the mermaid.

What could be luckier than a mermaid?

Keeper knew exactly what: a mermaid mama, who would know exactly how to help Keeper get out of the boatload of trouble that she had caused.

Exactly!

And in that late afternoon and early evening of mad-in-the-air and no-one-talking-to-Keeper, Keeper made a majorly big realization.

She had *heard* those crabs. No doubt about it. No matter how much practicality Signe invoked, those crabs had spoken to her.

If Keeper could hear crabs, didn't it stand to reckon that she could hear other sea creatures, too, like maybe *mermaids*? And if she could hear mermaids, wouldn't that mean that mermaids could hear *her*?

Exactly!

And so maybe, just maybe, *maybe maybe maybe*, she could find the only grown-up left who could help Keeper fix the world unto itself.

Her mother.

And right there she started cooking up a plan. Her perfect plan.

17

Keeper's perfect plan:

A. Wait until Signe is sound asleep.

B. Sneak out of the house with BD.

C. Get into *The Scamper*.

D. Wait for the tide to rise.

E. When the tide has risen, untie the knot.

F. Be extra sure that the tide is all the way up before untying the knot, or else the boat will go in the wrong direction.

G. Once the knot is untied, row across the pond toward the channel.

H. Go through the channel—it might be tight.

I. Row to the sandbar.

J. Find Meggie Marie.

K. Tell Meggie Marie everything that happened on this horrible day, *everything*.

L. Ask Meggie Marie what to do.

M. Wait for the tide to turn back around.

N. Row back through channel and across the pond.

O. Tie up *The Scamper*.

P. Sneak back into house.

Q. Do not wake up Signe.

R. Wake up early tomorrow morning so Signe won't suspect anything.

S–Z. Do whatever Meggie Marie says to do to fix everything.

Keeper smiled at BD. She had worked it all out. The sandbar was famous for its mermaids; plus, it was the last place she had seen her mother. If she was going to find Meggie Marie, it would be on the sandbar. De Vaca's Rock.

Meggie Marie knew everyone who lived on Oyster

Ridge Road. She would know how to fix things. She would know what would make Signe, Dogie, and Mr. Beauchamp happy again.

Also, if Keeper took *The Scamper*, she would not have to break her promise to Signe, the one she had made when she was three, the night Meggie Marie swam away. And what promise would that be? The one to not ever, ever, ever go swimming through those waves again.

By using the boat, Keeper could keep her promise. She would not be swimming. Nope. No breaststroke. No Australian crawl. No backstroke, either. None of that. She would be rowing. Keeper had not made any promises about rowing.

It was perfect, perfect, perfect.

"It's perfecto!" Keeper told BD, who was still under the bed.

To seal the deal, she wrote it all down, *Steps A–Z*, on a piece of notebook paper. Then she started to fold it up to put in her back pocket, but first she decided to memorize it, which was smart thinking because what if the paper got wet and all the ink washed off? And what if she got all the way to *Step G* and could not read *Step H*? Then what? Or how about if she mixed up *Steps B* and *P*? That would throw off everything.

So, for the next few hours, she stared at the plan and learned each step by heart: A, B, C, D, E, F, G, H, I, J, K, L, M, N, O, P, Q, R, S–Z. And to make it even better, she memorized it backward too. Just in case.

18

And now, all these hours later, here she was. In the boat, the notebook paper in her back pocket, putting her perfect plan into action. And so far, so good. *Steps A, B,* and *C* had gone swimmingly. When she and BD had tiptoed out the kitchen door barely an hour ago, BD hadn't made a single sound to wake up Signe. Somehow, he even managed to keep his toenails from clicking on the hard floor of the hallway.

Once outside, he had loped across the grassy lawn, right next to Keeper, quiet as a marsh mouse, stepped softly onto the wooden pier so as not to make any noise, then lowered himself down into the boat as lightly as a mosquito landing on a bare arm.

Dogie's boat. *The Scamper.*

Keeper did not have permission to use Dogie's

boat, did she? "It's okay," she told BD. "We'll be back *waaayyy* before Dogie wakes up." She knew that Dogie got up early to go open the Bus in time for the usual surfers who showed up to rent his surfboards or to buy a bar of wax. Surfers were early risers. Keeper knew this.

If her plan worked the way it was supposed to, then Dogie would never even know that she had taken the boat in the first place.

Speaking of the plan, it was good that she had memorized it because in all of this darkness, she surely couldn't read it. Whew! Good thinking, as Signe would say.

Keeper scanned the eastern horizon. "Where is the moon?" she asked the starry sky.

"Woof!" answered BD. Keeper knew that if BD could find the moon for her, he would. He'd grab it right out of the sky and hand it to her.

As Keeper sat there, she began to notice the noise of the tumbling waves on the other side of the sand dunes, a steady roar in the darkness. How could she have missed hearing them when they were always there?

And where the heck was that moon? Just then a soft breeze lifted over and circled around her head. There, on the wind's back, she heard it: *Keeper. Keeper.* She gripped the sides of the boat with her hands.

"Listen," she said to BD. The dog sat up and cocked his ears. The wind, as thin as paper, slipped by again.

Her name, the one her mother had given her seven years ago, right before she swam away. Ever since then, in all that time, Keeper had not heard one single word from Meggie Marie, not one. She leaned into the sound. *Keeper. Keeper.*

Then, just as quickly as it arose, the breeze vanished, leaving her name right there.

19

The Texas coast forms an arc, like a large rainbow, hugging the salty water of the Gulf of Mexico, laden with redfish and electric eels and speckled trout, cabbage heads and jellyfish and flounders. Right there, nestled between Galveston to the north and Corpus Christi to the south, right at the foot of a salt grass marsh, lies a narrow strip of quiet beach, isolated but for an oyster shell road that starts about ten miles inland in a tiny town called Tater.

But long before Tater, perhaps fifty thousand years ago, maybe longer, maybe a hundred thousand years ago, or even a million, a family of oysters built themselves a bed a hundred yards from the shore. It was a perfect place for the little oyster family. The water temperature was just right, the floor of the sea was solid, and the waves were gentle. Word soon spread in the oyster community, and it wasn't long before the small bed grew into a very large bed. Every year more and more oysters moved in, adding their newer shells to the older shells until the bed became wide and thick and also taller. As the oyster bed grew, the waves pushed sand and pebbles and grit up against it until it formed a long, narrow shoal just below the surface of the water. Over the centuries the waves pushed tons of sand and rocks and shells up against both sides of the oyster bed until it was completely covered over. The oysters eventually moved away and found other places for their beds, but they left behind their ancient shells, cemented together with all that sand and rocks and pebbles, creating a solid, permanent structure that geologists and oceanographers call a "sandbar," even though it was more like a big underwater rock than a pile of loose sand.

There it has rested, a hundred yards from shore, barely poking its noggin above the water. It is now known as De Vaca's Rock, named for the moment Álvar

Núñez Cabeza de Vaca sailed all the way from Spain and bumped right into it, gouging a rather large hole in the bottom of his ship in 1528, almost five hundred years ago. As soon as the ship listed, Cabeza de Vaca gathered his men and chickens and goats and swam to shore, and just as he did, he was greeted by a gathering of the resident coastal tribespeople known as the Karankawa.

The Karankawa tribe did not name the sandbar De Vaca's Rock. After all, his was not the first nor the last ship to scrape its hull against it. The Karankawas knew the sandbar for its older purpose, a meeting place for stingrays.

And tonight, this very night, the stingrays gathered there, just as they do each year when the midsummer moon is full, just as they had for thousands of years.

How many stingrays were there? A hundred? A thousand? More? They were waiting for the moonlight to guide them through the narrow channel called the Cut, right into the middle of the pond, its bottom thick and silty, perfect for their purposes. There, between the blades of the marsh grass that grew from the bottom, they'd lay their eggs. And when they were done, they'd use the waning light to return to the blue-green gulf, where they would swim out to deeper water. It was a ritual that the moon and the stingrays had performed for thousands of years, maybe millions.

Mermaids' purses. That's what their egg sacs are called.

Mermaids' purses.

Though it's not written in his captain's log, some believe that the reason Cabeza de Vaca ran his ship onto the sandbar in the first place was because of a sultry mermaid. It's easy enough to believe, especially when it's documented, right there in Cabeza de Vaca's own papers safe in a museum in Spain, where they've been for almost five hundred years, ever since he left the shores of Texas and arrived back in his homeland.

The sandbar was the last place that Keeper saw her mother, watched her swim away beneath a million stars. Just as gone as Cabeza de Vaca and the Karankawas. Gone.

20

Knee to paw, face-to-face, Keeper looked right at BD. "We can find her, boy. Easy peasy." With that, a small bit of happy raced through her.

BD pressed against her. Keeper breathed in his doggy smell, a mixture of Purina Dog Chow and Palmolive dish soap, the faint traces of his dinner and the bath she had given him a day or two ago, added to his own peculiar BD smell, something like garlic and sand and honey all mixed together.

Over BD's head she saw the outlines of the three dark houses, the only houses on Oyster Ridge Road. Resting atop their tall posts, they looked like shorebirds, their fat bodies standing on thin legs, tall enough to let the water slide beneath them during a storm.

Her own house, the one she shared with Signe, was the closest to the pond. In the daylight it was painted haint blue, a grayish shade, more gray than blue, but now, in the darkness, it looked like no color at all. In her room her empty bed waited, the cotton sheet shoved to the end of the mattress. And in the next room Signe slept, unaware that her girl and BD were out there on the pond, the two of them in *The Scamper*.

Thinking about Signe made that tiny bit of happy flitter a bit. "Shouldn't the moon be up by now?" Keeper asked.

"Moon!" she called, as if the sky could hear her. But there was no hurrying the moon. A girl who grows up with the tides coming and going knows that it takes the moon to pull the water out to sea. Which was where she needed to go. "Hurry up, you ol' moon," she said anyway. *Step D* was taking much longer than she had anticipated, and she still had lots of steps to go.

She drummed her fingers on the boat's sides, as if that might make the moon come up a little sooner.

BD thumped his tail. Keeper stopped drumming.

Farther along the bank, she could see the silhouettes of the sabal palms where Captain slept in his nest. Captain, their resident seagull.

Captain!

Another one of those wind gusts bumped against her. Some of today's mess was *his* fault. Yes, the talking crabs had started it. But Captain had caused his share of the trouble too. And now he was surely fast asleep up there in his palm tree.

Beyond Captain's palm, Keeper saw the faint glow of the crushed oyster shells on the road. She heard the rolling breakers of the surf on the other side of the sand dunes, the dunes that formed a rim around the Cut. The only thing that connected this pond to the gulf was a narrow channel, a ditch that sliced through the sand dunes and rose and fell with the tides, sending the water into the pond and then pulling it back out again. It was the pulling-back-out part that Keeper was waiting for.

Collectively, the back-and-forth pond and the

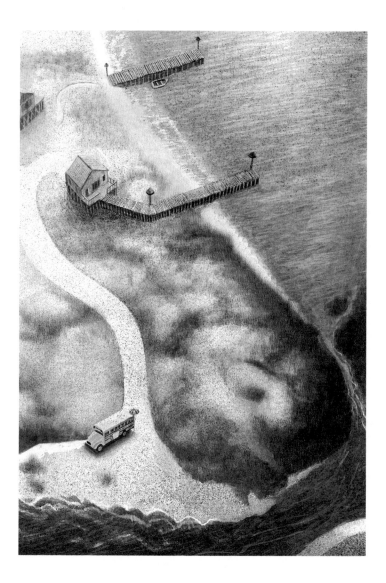

connecting channel were known by everyone on Oyster Ridge Road as "the Cut."

Everyone who mattered to Keeper lived here, along Oyster Ridge Road, with its dunes and salt grass marsh and oyster shell road and rolling surf: Signe and Dogie and Mr. Beauchamp. (They were all mad at her.) BD and Sinbad and Captain and Too—the beasts. (They weren't mad at her.)

The only one not here was Meggie Marie.

For Keeper's whole entire ten-year-long life, the world unto itself had been her home, her home with Signe and BD, and the long-legged sandpipers that scurried along the beach, and the sand dollars that lined her bedroom window, and the shrimp boats just behind the breakers, their nets like butterfly wings dipping into the water—everything she knew and cared about.

And today she had ruined it all.

21

The darkness all around her was deep. Stars, even a sky full of them, don't put out much light. Keeper's eyes had adjusted to the darkness a little, but even so, she wished there were more light. Where, oh where, was the moon?

If she had checked Dogie's tidal chart before she came out here . . . but of course, she couldn't have even if she'd thought of it, because even though Dogie said he wasn't mad, she knew he *had* to be . . . all because of her and Captain and BD and, well, Too as well, don't forget Too, he was also to blame.

Of course Dogie was mad.

Keeper sighed. So even if she'd thought of the chart, she wouldn't have asked Dogie for it anyway, as she was quite sure Dogie didn't want to see her.

Still, she wished she'd checked the chart. Sometimes knowing how long you had to wait for something made the waiting easier.

And Keeper knew about waiting.

She jiggled her legs impatiently and felt the little carving in her pocket bump against her thigh.

She hadn't intended to bring Yemaya with her, but just as she was sneaking out of her room, she saw the little figurine, right there in a row with six others. Seven of them altogether. There was that lucky number again. Seven merlings. All of them given to her by Mr. Beauchamp.

"I'll bring you with me . . . for luck," she'd said to them with her quietest voice. Then she scooped the six into a shoe box and put Yemaya, her favorite, in her pocket and slipped down the hall.

Now Keeper felt BD lick her knees. "Enough with the stealth kisses, you," she whispered. He thumped his tail against the bottom of the boat.

BD had been only a roly-poly puppy when Meggie Marie left. Would he recognize her when he saw her?

Keeper was counting on him to help find her.

Meggie Marie.

For seven years Keeper had waited for her mother. Often she had stood at the water's edge and looked out, searched the tops of waves, scanned the horizon. But even though Keeper had waited for Meggie Marie, she had not needed her.

After all, she had Signe. Signe with her spiky white hair and her practical ways and her ability to mend a seagull's broken wing. But now, on this dark night, Signe was furious with her.

Now Keeper needed Meggie Marie. Needing was stronger than waiting.

"If we can't find her . . ." Keeper let the sentence trail off into the damp air. Where was that moon?

22

Keeper and BD were not the only ones out in the deep dark night at that moment. Mr. Beauchamp and his one-eyed cat Sinbad were sitting on their porch, waiting for the moon to rise. The old man slumped in his rocking chair, his eyes closed in a troubled sleep. He and Sinbad had been waiting for this moon too, waiting for it to shine down on the night-blooming cyrus and urge their enormous blossoms to break open.

Now the old man gasped for a breath as he slept. Sinbad rubbed against his master's thin leg, pressed the side of his face against his bony shin.

From where Sinbad sat, he heard the old man's breath rattle in his chest. With each of the man's raspy inhales and exhales, a deep lonesome inched its way just beneath the cat's fur. He and Mr. Beauchamp had been together for such a long time, and now the cat knew that the old man didn't have much longer.

Sinbad blinked his one eye and hoisted himself onto the porch rail. He scanned the starry sky. Sometimes a blue moon, he knew, took her time. He raised a front paw and gave it a good lick. Then he looked out across the pond toward the spot where the small boat was tied up at the dock.

Ahoy! What was this? From his perch, Sinbad could see the girl and the dog. *Blow me down!* thought the cat. What were the girl and the dog doing out this late? In the boat? Alone? Shouldn't someone be with them? He looked around. There were no lights on in the other two houses.

He looked out toward the pond again. The tide was coming in, lifting the boat higher against the dock. He hoped the rope held. Otherwise, as soon as the moon rose, the water would pull the boat and the dog and the girl with it, through the channel and straight out to sea.

To sea? Sinbad had his own memories of seafaring,

not all of them pleasant. He scratched the rail of the porch with his sharp claws. Maybe he should alert someone? Yes, that would be a good idea. The cat took a deep breath and prepared to let out a big *meeooowwww*, when, from the corner of his one good eye, he saw a glimmer of light coming from the boat.

Flick!

What was that?

Flick!

There it was again. Had the girl struck a match?

Flick!

He blinked his eye.

No. It couldn't be. Not after all these years.

Flick!

But what else could it be? The glow was unmistakable. A *porte-bonheur!* It was hanging on a ribbon around her neck. Could it be the same one? Or was it another? Surely this was it. But how had the girl come to get such a lucky charm, for what else could it be?

A *porte-bonheur* was extremely rare, and if this was the same one, it had been missing for a very long time. He slipped off the porch rail and curled up in Mr. Beauchamp's lap. The worry in his belly loosened its grip a tiny bit. Maybe the girl could find . . . but no . . . it'd been too many years . . . it wasn't possible . . . was it? . . . a dozen cat's lives had passed since . . . still . . . it *was* a lucky charm . . . so maybe . . .

Just maybe.

He made a good-luck wish for the girl and the dog: *Find the one who's been missing.* It was a good wish, as shiny as the cat's good eye. Then he purred for the reluctant moon.

23

Just as Keeper let herself worry for just the slightest nanosecond about finding her mother, a better thought came to her. She had her lucky charm. And now that she thought about it, she also knew exactly *why* her mother had given it to her: *So she will recognize me when she sees me!*

Exactly!

And if the charm wasn't lucky enough, Keeper had the seven carved figurines as backup.

Mr. Beauchamp was an expert on the merrow, those watery creatures who are half fish or dolphin or seal and half human.

"Find a body of water," Mr. Beauchamp had told Keeper, "and you will likely find a merstory." Keeper loved that. Merstory. The history of the merpeople.

And Mr. Beauchamp was full of merstories, dozens of them, and he shared them all with Keeper.

Mr. Beauchamp was not her real grandfather, but he might as well have been. He did all sorts of grandfatherly things: told her stories, taught her how to play checkers, sang old sea chanteys to her. Things Keeper figured grandfathers did.

And above all, he carved the merlings for her.

As the boat rocked with the lifting tide, Keeper reached beneath the bench for the shoe box and lifted the lid. She had stuffed one of her old SHOP AT THE BUS T-shirts, a purple one, down in the bottom of the box so that her merlings would be cozy and warm. Even in the dark, she could tell them apart. Her fingers were familiar with each carving's expression, each groove, each tiny scale.

After all, she had found each of them *before* Mr. Beauchamp had carved them. It wasn't something she learned. She just seemed to know. And why not? Shouldn't a girl who was part mer herself know how to find the little mer spirits in the wood?

She'd never forget the first one, a siren. She had been walking along the beach with Signe and BD, right at the water's edge, when something bumped against her foot.

"Yikes!" She jumped. She was afraid it was a crab.

But when she looked down, she saw the thick chunk of gray wood. She nudged it with her toe. It was solid, scarred from its tumbles with the seashells and rocks that had likely traveled with it on its journey to this beach. BD sniffed it and barked. *Toss it, toss it.*

BD loved to play fetch, and there was always plenty of driftwood for a quick game. But when she picked up this particular piece, she felt a buzz run through her fingertips. She moved it to her other hand. Yes. The wood was buzzing. She stared at it. It was heavier than most of the sticks and bits of lumber that usually washed ashore.

"It's got substance," said Signe.

Keeper looked at the wood again, then for some reason she couldn't explain, she held it up to her ear. She caught her breath. It was humming.

"A siren!" she said. Signe looked at her.

"Keeper," Signe said, "it's just a piece of wood."

Keeper knew that Signe didn't put much stock in merstories. Signe was all business. But Signe's reasonableness didn't matter to Keeper. She took the chunk of wood directly to Mr. Beauchamp, held it out to him, and said, "A siren."

The siren was the first merling that Mr. Beauchamp carved for her. After that, she found six others:

1. Sedna, the goddess of the Arctic seas;
2. the *ningyo*, all the way from Japan;
3. the *Meerfrau*, whose apron was always wet;
4. Lorelei, who fell in love with stranded sailors;
5. the *rusalka*, the trickster; and last of all:
6. Yemaya . . . the big mama of all the waters—
7. Seven in all with the singing siren.

"Gifts," Mr. Beauchamp had said. Keeper loved them completely, loved that they had found her on the beach, loved that she had found them in the wood, loved that Mr. Beauchamp uncovered each one with the strokes of his carving knife, loved that there were no two alike, loved that she was the only one in the whole wide world to have her very own tribe of merlings.

She had spent hours and hours playing with them. She made sand villages for them, including castles and caves and even a mer-diner, where they could order up the itsy-bitsy clams that Keeper scooped out of the wet sand. At night she lined them up on the edge of the bathtub when she took a bath. She set them in a semicircle beside her plate at dinner. She took them with her everywhere, in her pockets, in her backpack, in a shoe box.

And now here they were in *The Scamper* with her, Mr. Beauchamp's gifts to her, which, if her plan worked, would now be her gifts to someone else.

Just in case.

"Double insurance" is what Signe would call it. Seven pieces of double insurance.

Yep, her plan was a good one. Plus, to seal the deal,

she had seven merlings. Seven gifts. For Yemaya. Big mama of the ocean. Of all the merpeople, Yemaya was the most important. The others were all unique in their own ways, but it was only Yemaya who had special powers.

She wasn't pretty like Lorelei, nor did she sing like the sirens, but Mr. Beauchamp had told Keeper, "If you give her a gift, she might grant a wish."

Between the charm and Yemaya and all those sevens, how much more luck could she possibly have?

And not only that, she had her perfect plan, all written out, stuffed into her back pocket and memorized, too.

"Cooleoleo!" she said, a word she had picked up from the surfers, one of her favorite words of all time.

BD planted a stealth kiss right on her cheek.

24

But right now the perfect plan was stuck until the moon finished lifting up the tide. Otherwise, the boat wasn't going anywhere. Keeper couldn't keep her legs still. She bounced them up and down, up and down, up and down. She could tell that the water was rising, but not fast enough for her. She also knew that she had to wait until the tide was *completely* up, or else it would pull her in the wrong direction, right into the salt grass marsh, exactly the opposite direction of where she needed to go.

BD whined, *Please, let's go home, please.*

He sincerely wanted to go back to his spot beside Keeper's bed.

"You know, BD, this is your fault too," she told him. Then Keeper felt bad for saying that. It wasn't really his fault, was it?

But it was *kind of* his fault. He did, after all, chase the cat.

"Sinbad's fault too!" she announced. The cat was partly to blame, for sure. Darned old cat.

Thinking about the cat reminded Keeper of Mr. Beauchamp again. Lately, he spent more and more time sitting on his porch with Sinbad, staring out at the water. He got up only a few times a day to eat and tend to his flowers and feed the cat. Once a week or so, Dogie drove him into town to get his groceries and cat food, but aside from that, he rarely left his house.

"All the more reason for us to check on him," Signe had told Keeper. And they did. Signe, Keeper, and Dogie all visited him every single day. Keeper took her merlings with her and listened to him tell her their stories while she watered his potted plants.

But now the thought of Mr. Beauchamp made a ball of guilt clump up in the back of her throat.

Mr. Beauchamp was the oldest person on Oyster Ridge Road, so old that he told Keeper he had forgotten his date of birth.

"Barnacles!" he told her. "Old as barnacles." Besides the merstories, he had taught her how to sing sea chanteys, which she in turn taught Dogie and which none of them sang for Signe, because, well, Signe, they knew, would say, "Is that appropriate?" and if Keeper were being honest, she would have to say that while *she* didn't think anything was wrong with them, they did, she had to admit, have a few words in them that were even more supercharged than "stupid," so it was highly likely that Signe would fail to admire them the same way that Keeper, Mr. Beauchamp, and Dogie did, so the chanteys were not sung for Signe.

Mr. Beauchamp also showed Keeper how to care for the antique roses and the night-blooming cyrus that he grew in large porcelain pots on his porch.

He told her, "Cyrus only bloom once a year, and only when the moon is full." And then he would grow very still and stare out at the water, almost as though he disappeared somewhere inside his head. Keeper always knew not to disturb him when he did that.

"He must have wonderful memories," Signe had

told her once, when Keeper had asked her why Mr. Beauchamp disappeared in his head like that sometimes.

Every year, each July, they all waited for the full moon to cast her beams across his porch and urge the magical blossoms to burst open.

Like Keeper, Mr. Beauchamp was waiting for someone, someone who might appear when the cyrus opened its huge petals and released its spicy scent into the nighttime air. And every year Mr. Beauchamp told Keeper, "This could be the year, *mon petite*."

And this year, especially, with Mr. Beauchamp looking older than the oldest of barnacles, Keeper had hoped that whoever he was waiting for would finally arrive, just in time for the blooms on the cyrus.

And then, that very morning, in one fast, too-too fast, horribly fast moment, Keeper had taken her eye off of BD, who was as fast as a streaking bullet, even though Signe had warned her: keep an eye on the dog.

So, really, it *was* all Keeper's fault.

And that wasn't even all of what had happened that

got her into so much trouble that morning. "Stupid crabs!" she stewed from her perch on the boat's bench. And also, where the heck was that stupid moon?

"Woof," woofed BD. His tongue washed her knee again.

"Shhhh." Keeper shushed him. Her heart thumped against her rib cage in a chant: *Hurry, hurry, hurry.*

25

Boy, it's dark out, Keeper thought. She could barely make out the dim outlines of the shaggy palm trees along the edge of the Cut. Captain was up in one of them, just yards away, snuggled into his nest. Keeper didn't know anyone else who had a resident seagull. How great was that? And they'd had one for five years—ever since that night when Captain had crash-landed into their kitchen window. A storm had blown up, and the wind had caught him. *Smack!* He tumbled right into their windowpane, sending glass and feathers flying across the kitchen floor.

Keeper had almost jumped out of her skin. "Yikes!" she hollered. *Ssscccrrrrreeeeeeeeeeeeccccchhhhhhhhh!!!!* The seagull squawked and squawked. Keeper screamed again. And BD barked like a crazy dog, "Woofwoof-

woofwoofwoof!!!" then stood beneath the kitchen table and growled.

In the midst of it all, Signe, calm as always, managed to catch the bird by throwing a dish towel over him and tucking him underneath her arm. Then she held his beak shut with her hand and yelled at Keeper, "Find the tape!" Keeper quit howling, and after a brief rummaging through the junk drawer beside the washing machine, she found the tape, a sticky roll of gray tape that Signe called "duck tape." Keeper lifted it out of the drawer. Would duck tape work on seagulls? She handed it to Signe.

"Seagull tape," Keeper said. Signe smiled, but she was still all business. Signe was always all business, which could be a good thing when you have a scared-to-death seagull tucked under your arm and a growling-like-mad dog under your table.

That was the thing about Signe, Keeper now thought. Hardly anything ever ruffled her feathers, which was why today had been so, so terrible. Keeper looked back at the palm trees. All she could see were their quiet shadows. She couldn't see Captain at all.

Keeper thought about that night again. Once Signe had gotten the bird to calm down and shushed BD at the same time, Signe wrapped the gull's damaged wing in a dishcloth and pin it so that he couldn't flap the wing and reinjure himself.

"There," she'd said when she was finished, and handed the gull to Keeper.

Keeper felt the bird shaking in her hands. She stroked his soft feathers and cooed to him. "Cooleo-leo," she said quietly, mostly because she didn't really know what else to say, but also because the very fact that she was holding a seagull in her arms was definitely cooleoleo. And while Keeper held him, Signe took the duck (seagull) tape off of the seagull's beak. Then she made him a warm bowl of oatmeal, which seemed to make his shivers ease up a little. Afterward Keeper set him on the floor and watched as he hopped underneath the table and settled right next to BD, which surprised everyone, including BD. From then on, Captain thought he was a member of the family.

Family. This was something Keeper thought about a lot.

None of the residents of Oyster Ridge Road were actually related to one another. Dogie was not her father, even though she wished he were her father. Mr. Beauchamp was not her grandfather, even though he seemed like a grandfather. And Signe? She was *not* Keeper's mother.

Still, Signe was right there, in Keeper's earliest memories. Actually, Signe was in *all* of her memories. And yes, Keeper remembered bits and pieces of Meggie Marie. She remembered her long hair, so like her own and so unlike Signe's short spikes. She remembered Meggie Marie's voice. "Ch-ch-chiming," that's how Dogie described it, "l-l-like bells." Signe's voice was quieter, not at all like bells. And mostly, Keeper remembered that Meggie Marie was always laughing. To Meggie Marie, everything was funny, and she usually made everyone else laugh too, even Signe.

Keeper remembered laughing with Meggie Marie.

But Meggie Marie had left. And Signe hadn't.

Signe had stayed.

And every night when Signe tucked Keeper into bed, she had kissed her on the forehead and said, "You and me, Sweet Pea. You and me." And every night for seven years, it had not mattered so much that Meggie Marie had turned into her mermaid self and disappeared beneath the waves. Because of Signe, the world unto itself had been cooleoleo.

Until today.

Today, when everything went wrong.

Today, when everything was ruined.

Today, when, for the second time ever in Keeper's whole entire life, Signe started crying.

26

The power of Signe's crying dug at Keeper.

Signe crying.

Signe crying.

Signe crying.

Now a fear as deep as the ocean zipped through Keeper's body, her biggest fear ever, one so deep, she knew not to ever, ever say it out loud, not ever. And then today, it crawled out of her like an ugly toad: If a girl's own mother can swim away, what would keep everyone else from leaving too, especially if that same girl caused so much trouble? The toad of fear made a big, fat *cccrrooaaaakkkk* right in Keeper's stomach.

Where was the blasted moon?

Keeper tested *The Scamper*'s rope. It was still too taut to loosen the knot. But it was close. Another inch, she reckoned, and the rope would finally slacken, whereupon *Step D* would turn into *Steps E* and *F*. She didn't know how long it took the water in the pond to rise an inch.

Dogie would. Dogie knew all about tides and how fast they rose and fell.

She'd have to remember to ask him about it.

Once he got over being mad.

Which depended entirely upon her fixing things.

Sigh.

"Come on, moon," she said, adding a "Grrrr . . ." of frustration.

"Grrrr . . . ," added BD, halfheartedly.

One would think that a dog who has lived his whole life by the water would not worry too much about that same water. But BD was not of the retriever ilk. Not a Labrador. Not a golden. Not a spaniel. He was *not* bred for paddling through the waves or jumping into a lake or swimming across a pond. He didn't even enjoy a bath, which Keeper gave him once a week.

No-siree-bob, water was not BD's native country. And in the small boat there was only a thin plank or two between himself and a whole lot of water. *Pleeeeeaaasssseeeee, let's go back,* he whined. "Woof," he said.

Right then, in the middle of BD's woof, a wave came out of nowhere and rolled under them. It pushed the boat against the pier, made it squeak as it rubbed the wooden beams. BD's voice matched the boat's squeak. *Please, please, please.*

Then, as quickly as the rolling wave came, it disappeared. The water smoothed itself out and turned quiet again. Keeper couldn't see anything on the water but the tiny glimmers of the stars reflecting back up at her.

But when she turned toward the pier, she realized that the boat had inched up against it. The rope, too, had gathered some slack.

"Yesyesyesyes!"

She punched her fists into the air, and, well, she just

couldn't help it, the lines of one of Mr. Beauchamp's sea chanteys slipped right out of her:

"Hey ho, and up she rises
Hey ho, and up she rises
Hey ho, and up she rises
Early in the morning . . ."

And as if the sea heard her, another wave rolled under the boat and lifted it another inch.

27

Keeper gave her charm a happy tug. Her lucky charm. It was working! The ribbon it hung from was smooth as silk, a bright pink ribbon that Signe had brought home one day and tied around Keeper's ponytail.

Keeper remembered the day Signe dug it out of the grocery bags resting on the kitchen table. She held it up, the pink so pink that Keeper had to squint at first.

"Just because," said Signe.

That was unusual. Signe rarely did anything "just because."

Keeper knew that the ribbon was an extravagance for Signe, an added expense that she didn't need.

But while Keeper stood there in the kitchen, Signe

had brushed Keeper's long, black hair and tied the pink ribbon around it, startling in its pinkness, so pink against her black hair.

"A new ribbon for my old girl," said Signe.

Keeper was surprised by Signe's use of the word "old."

"Is ten old?" she asked.

For a moment Signe had not answered, but then, as she finished tying the bow, she whispered, "Older than BD's lifetime." That was true—BD was younger than Keeper, at least in human years. But he was older than her in dog years, forty-nine if you counted in canine. In fact, if you went by dog years, BD was older than Signe, who was twenty-five. Keeper had no idea how old Dogie was. And no one was as old as Mr. Beauchamp.

Then she turned to Signe and asked, "Is ten old for a mermaid?"

Signe looked at her and said, "That is a question for the universe." Whenever Signe did not want to give Keeper a straight answer, that's how she replied—"It's a question for the universe"—and left it like that, as if the universe knew.

Keeper had noticed that most of her questions about mermaids, which included questions about Meggie Marie, were answered by Signe in this same way.

Keeper had reached behind her head to feel the satin ribbon between her fingers, as soft as her very own hair. She hadn't been ten for very long, only a few days, but she liked the roundness of the number, the way it used up all of her fingers or all of her toes, depending upon which way she was counting.

"Stealth kiss," Keeper had told Signe, and given her a quick kiss on the cheek.

"Take care of it," Signe had said, smiling.

"I will," Keeper had promised.

She had set the ribbon on top of her dresser, where it glowed amidst her collection of merlings. The seven of them. It was right there when Keeper dug the charm out from the pile of socks in her top drawer earlier that day. The old chain, rusty and stiff, had snapped in her hands, so she slipped the disk off of it and dropped the chain back into the drawer, then threaded the ribbon through the loop on top of the charm.

Now Keeper stopped tugging. She didn't want to break the ribbon and lose the charm, the only gift she remembered her mother ever giving her. Keeper remembered three things from that night:

1. Her mother's laughing voice, singing in her ear, "Happy Birthday, little mergirl"
2. The golden charm
3. Her mother calling to her as she swam away: *"Keeper. Keeper."*

Over and over. Her name had come in circles around her ears. It made her dizzy. Signe had held on to her then, held her tight, while Meggie Marie slipped farther and farther into the dark waves. Keeper had reached as far as she could toward her, but Signe wouldn't let her go.

Keeper. Keeper.

That's what Keeper remembered from such a long time ago.

And something else Keeper remembered from that night: Signe crying.

28

When a girl is born in the sea, she knows about cabbage heads and kingfishers. She knows about starfish and seaweed and sand. She knows about oysters and salt grass and sun perch. All of these things.

Signe knew about things too, even though she was not born in the sea. She knew how to braid Keeper's hair to keep it off her neck. She knew how to wrap a seagull's broken wing in a kitchen towel and how to pluck sandburs out of BD's fur. She knew about helping old Mr. Beauchamp climb the steps up to his house even when he said he didn't need the help. And she knew about sitting on the porch in the evenings with Dogie and watching the night settle over them. She knew when to take an extra shift at the Prince

Oyster Bar and Bar whenever she could so that she could buy a pink ribbon for her girl.

What she did not know? That Keeper was out in the boat in the middle of the night.

29

As the water beneath *The Scamper* rose, another rolling wave bumped against her, this one stronger than the last. The boat rocked, then nudged against the pier again, and this time BD barked at it.

Keeper rubbed his ears. *"Shhhh,"* she told him. "It's only the tide." Even though he wasn't convinced, he settled back down at her feet.

Poor BD, she thought. He was no sailor dog. Not like Sinbad, who, according to Mr. Beauchamp, had sailed the seven seas.

"He comes from a long line of pirate cats," he'd declared.

BD had never sailed any seas. "Sinbad!" Keeper grumped. Then she looked at BD and pronounced, "He's a wax wart," which was surfer language for a majorly big bump in the wax on a surfboard. Sure, the wax needed to be bumpy, but if it had a great big bump in the wrong place, that was a wax wart.

Sinbad had definitely been a wax wart that day. She said it again: "He's a wax wart."

She wanted to be angry at the old cat, but it was hard to be upset for too long with a cat who had only one eye, which at turns was either blue or green depending upon the season or the occasion. And sometimes, on cloudy days, it might even be gray.

No. Keeper wasn't angry at Sinbad. Or BD. Or Captain, either, even though all three of them were party to the destruction.

However, crabs? She was not at all happy with the crabs. "Stupid crabs!"

And Mr. Beauchamp, she knew, was not happy with anyone.

Keeper rubbed her bare knees poking out from her shorts. Her fingers traced the knobby outlines of her kneecaps. She had studied her knees a million times. Mermaids did not have knees. Keeper did. Her knees

CHILDREN'S ROOM

were right there. Thinking about her knees reminded her of Mr. Beauchamp kneeling over his flowers, which in turn reminded her of Dogie with his ukulele, and that reminded her of Signe. Crying.

This had been the worst day ever.

30

It was bad enough that the wooden bowl had broken, but the gumbo pot was ruined too. Keeper had spent a good hour scrubbing and scrubbing at the black gunk in the bottom of the pot. Her fingers were pruny, her arms ached from scrubbing so hard, and her newest T-shirt, the electric pink Dogie T-shirt that read SHOP AT THE BUS, was soaking wet and smelled like gumbo. No, make that *burnt* gumbo.

But no matter how hard Keeper scrubbed, she could not get all the gunk out of the bottom. Finally, she threw the brush in the sink. She felt terrible about the gumbo and the bowl. And clearly the pot was ruined too. Signe's gumbo pot. Ack! Keeper wiped her face with the bottom of her T-shirt. She could still smell the newness of it underneath the burnt gumbo.

She looked at her pruny fingers. They were sore from scrubbing. She pushed her hair back behind her ears. She wiped the sweat off her lip. The room still smelled like the ruined gumbo, sharp and dense. What a mess!

She grabbed a kitchen towel and dried her hands, and just then, Signe walked into the kitchen, followed by BD. He had finally decided to come out from under the bed. He walked over to Keeper and leaned against her.

Keeper wanted to tell Signe, *Sorry. I'm so sorry for ruining the gumbo,* but her throat wouldn't cooperate. Maybe if she explained about how the crabs had talked to her first . . . But before she could get anything out, she heard Signe say, "You need to go to the Bus and tell Dogie about the crabs, Keeper."

Keeper closed her eyes. She knew that Signe was right, but the thought of what Dogie's face would look like when she told him that she had set the crabs free made her queasy.

She heard Signe say it again. "Tell Dogie about

the crabs." Then, to Keeper's dismay, Signe pressed her fingers against her eyes and said in the smallest voice imaginable, "Tonight was supposed to be just right . . . and now . . ."

A silence so thick Keeper could have punched it with her fist filled the kitchen. Even the sunlight streaming in through the window seemed to dim as it entered the room, muted by such a thick quiet. Keeper didn't know what to do. She stood on one leg, then the other. She did not want to tell Dogie about the crabs.

And then, from outside the screen door, came a familiar cry. "C'mon, c'mon!" It was Captain. At the sound of the bird's cry, BD wagged his tail. "Woof, woof!" He walked to the door and looked over his shoulder at Keeper who looked back at Signe. Signe crossed her arms.

Signe, Captain, and BD. All three of them were ganging up. There was no getting out of it. Keeper *had* to tell Dogie about the crabs. Shoot!

"Okay, okay," she said. "I'm going."

But as she and BD stepped out the door, she heard Signe say one more thing: "Keep an eye on the dog! Whatever you do, don't let him chase Sinbad."

"Woof!" barked BD. Keeper followed him, his tail in the air like a flag. And just above them, flying in wide circles, Captain.

"C'mon, c'mon!"

31

Once outside, Keeper sat on the bottom step and tied her sneakers. She was in no hurry to tell Dogie what had happened.

She felt the familiar sting of a sand flea bite on the side of her ankle. She should have put on a pair of socks. Sand fleas couldn't bite through socks. She needed a Dr Pepper. She needed to tell Dogie about the crabs.

The Bus wasn't that far from the haint blue house. A hundred yards, tops. Dogie kept an ice chest filled with Dr Peppers. She wondered if he would let her have one, just like he always did, once he heard about the crabs.

Signe never let her have soft drinks. "All they are is sugar," she said, as if sugar were a bad thing. Keeper liked sugar, but if you listened to Signe, you'd think that sugar was the same as an oil spill or something, and could ruin coastlines, along with her health. So the Dr Peppers were a secret between herself and Dogie, and besides, now that she was his official waxwing, she counted her Dr Peppers as part of her salary, even though she couldn't keep one in her red purse like she could the rest of her earnings. And thinking about the purse with its $42.00 reminded her that Signe had told her to save it for a rainy day, but there wasn't any rain in sight, and there also wasn't any blue moon gumbo in sight, and it was all because of those "stupid, stupid crabs!" which she needed to tell Dogie about, and geez, Louise . . .

Her stomach rumbled. She realized she had not had breakfast. Or lunch for that matter. A tiny empty spot opened up inside of her. She wasn't really hungry. But the Dr Pepper started sounding better and better, and maybe Dogie would only be a little bit mad and still let her have one. She stood up and walked across the yard, followed by BD.

And then . . . from across the road, she heard the familiar sound of Sinbad, his deep-throated meow slipping into her ear. "Meeeeooooowwwww!"

32

"Keep an eye on the dog." Six little words. Keep. An. Eye. On. The. Dog.

But as Keeper had walked out onto the steps with BD and Captain, to go tell Dogie about the crabs, as soon as she remembered the $42.00 she'd saved, she started thinking that maybe, yes, just *maybe*, she could repay Signe for the broken bowl.

Would $42.00 cover the cost of the bowl? She knew it was enough for a man's corduroy jacket. Corduroy jacket? Keeper didn't think one word about BD, much less six.

"C'mon, c'mon!" Captain! He was flying in broad circles over the houses.

As she watched him in his semicircular flight, her eye settled on Mr. Beauchamp's antique roses. They were in full bloom, brilliant in the warm salty air. Keeper felt a flush of pride over her role in caring for the roses. The roses were just like those that grew in his birthplace, French roses! He had shown her how to prune them, instructed her in how to give them just the right amount of bonemeal and how much water to pour into their beautiful pots.

"Keeper of the flowers," he had called her.

As she admired the bright orange and pink roses, a small bud of hope rose up inside of Keeper. Maybe if she asked him, Mr. Beauchamp would let her have a couple of them to take to Signe. Roses would make her feel better.

But just as Keeper began to cross the road, Sinbad hopped onto the rail and arched his back. He began to spit and glare at them with his one good eye.

Hardly anything looked as menacing as Sinbad's good eye, especially when he began to hiss and spit, like he was doing now.

According to Mr. Beauchamp, Sinbad was the last

of his line, the last of the great pirate cats. His great-great-great-great-great-great-great grandmother and grandfather had sailed with the notorious French privateer Jean Lafitte back in the early 1800s. That's what Mr. Beauchamp said.

Who knows why they were all born with only a single eye? Some say it helped them focus on the task at hand. It's true that if you're trying to look hard at something—something like a rat, say—you might close one eye, the better to zero in on your prey. Maybe those pirate cats spent so much time closing one eye that, eventually, they put all their sight into the single open one.

It didn't matter to Keeper that Sinbad had one eye or that he was a descendant of pirates.

What mattered was that he loved to taunt BD, which led to crazy, wild chases, chases in which things got knocked over and turned upside down. Something about Sinbad's hissing and spitting made BD go stark raving nutso.

But that morning Keeper's mind was not on Sinbad

or BD, either. She was just thinking about how beautiful the antique roses were and how surely they'd make Signe feel better.

And just as soon as she got the flowers and took them to Signe, she would then go tell Dogie about the crabs. He would understand. She just knew it. Then the world unto itself would be restored to its rightful order.

She was so busy thinking about the crabs and the flowers and Dogie that for a moment she did not notice—*really* notice—what Sinbad was up to.

One mistake. That's all it took. One taking-her-eye-off-of-the-dog second, and that did it. In less time than it took to blink, she got the picture. She got it just before it happened.

"Oh no," she said.

Too late.

BD. Short for Best Dog, but right then, short for Bad Dog.

Captain. Short for Pep Squad.

Sinbad. Short for Menace. Whose most fun game was to

  tease . . .

    BD, whose chasing switch was
    tripped, which
      stirred up . . .
        all sorts of . . .
          MAYHEM!!!

Mayday! Mayday! Mayday!

All at once, it was BD in full chase mode, heading straight after Sinbad while Captain cheered from the sidelines, "C'mon, c'mon!" Keeper saw Sinbad crouch between Mr. Beauchamp's pots of fragile roses and the exotic night-blooming cyrus. Maybe BD wouldn't see him. Maybe she could catch him in time.

MaybeMaybeMaybe . . .

But BD was too fast. He raced right by her, raced right up the porch steps, raced right through the fragile roses and the scraggly cyrus, the flowers that

Mr. Beauchamp loved, placed precariously close to the edge of the porch, which sat ten feet off the ground, too high for flowering plants to survive tipping over.

Still, Keeper yelled, "No, BD. Nooooo!!!!"

CRASH! BANG! SMASH!

Keeper froze at the bottom of the porch, a whole barrelful of "oh no's" filling up her throat and lungs and chest. Pot by pot, Mr. Beauchamp's beautiful flowers, his enchanted night-bloomers, his orange and pink antique roses, crashed onto the oyster shell driveway. Keeper didn't wait for them to finish falling before she ran onto the porch, two steps at a time, and grabbed BD's collar. His tail wagged, his tongue hung out. His fur stood straight up on his head.

She could swear he was smiling.

On the porch rail Sinbad calmly licked his paws.

Keeper tugged on BD's collar. She needed to get him off of the porch before . . . but too late.

Mr. Beauchamp opened the door. Keeper froze again. Two seconds later she heard Mr. Beauchamp cry out, "Ohh . . . !"

With a yank, Keeper pulled BD down the steps, Mr. Beauchamp close behind. And there, at the bottom, the beloved plants lay scattered, shattered. She couldn't move. BD leaned against her. She wanted to let go of the dog and hug Mr. Beauchamp, so like a grandfather only not her grandfather, but she felt stuck, glued to the ground.

All she could do was hold on to BD and watch as Mr. Beauchamp knelt down over his prized flowers.

And then, out of nowhere, Signe appeared, her face a storm cloud, her white hair blinding in the morning heat. And for some reason, Mr. Beauchamp pointed right at her, right at Signe, as if it were all Signe's fault, when it wasn't Signe's fault at all. Signe had told her, "Keep an eye on the dog." Six simple words.

Keeper watched as Signe walked right past her and reached for Mr. Beauchamp, bent over and shaking, watched as Signe helped him slowly walk back up the stairs, where she sat next to him on the porch, watched as Mr. Beauchamp leaned back in his old rocking chair, his face a map of sorrow.

Then she heard the old sailor, so much like a grandfather, tell Signe, in the saddest voice imaginable, "Stop waiting, *mon amie*, stop waiting." Tears streamed down both of their faces.

33

Waiting. It was so hard to do. Keeper had written the word "wait" on *Step D*: *Wait for the tide to rise.* But she had no idea the waiting would be this long. Now, as she sat in *The Scamper*, she considered screaming at the moon to make it hurry up. But that would just wake up Signe, which was not at all in the plan. See *Step A*.

Keeper did not think she could bear to see Signe's mad face again so soon. Or Signe's sad face, either. Signe crying. Was there anything worse?

Well, yes.

Yes, as a matter of fact, there was. Signe yelling. That seemed a lot worse. But then again, Signe crying . . .

And then there was Dogie's face . . .

Keeper covered her own face with both of her hands. Dogie's face had been more than sad. It was crushed . . . like the flowers . . . like the . . .

At the exact moment that Mr. Beauchamp had pointed at Signe, Keeper had taken off. She had run and run and run, straight to the Bus, BD right at her side.

"Here's my g-g-g-girl," Dogie had said as she and BD came in for a landing. Dogie's cheerfulness felt strange in the midst of so much chaos. Keeper looked down. She needed to tell him. She took a deep breath, but she was afraid that if she uttered a sound, she would start to cry, so she just nodded.

Dogie reached into the ice chest and pulled out a bottle of Dr Pepper and handed it to her. Without looking into his face, Keeper took the icy cold bottle in one hand and, with the other, pushed her hair behind her ear.

Then she watched as Dogie lifted both arms like an orchestra conductor and said to the dogs, "B-b-be off, b-b-beasts!" And with that, BD and Too took off down the beach in a streak, with Captain flying just above them.

Keeper swallowed a big swig of the icy drink. It burnt as it slid down her throat, and she wished now that she had eaten a bowl of cereal instead of releasing the crabs.

Crabs.

And roses.

And night-blooming cyrus.

And Signe's broken bowl.

And Mr. Beauchamp, bent over and trembling.

Signe crying.

She needed to tell Dogie about all of this.

She took another long drink of Dr Pepper, postponing everything as long as she could. But before she even finished swallowing, Dogie pulled out his ukulele and began to sing. *"Marry me, marry me."* He grinned at her conspiratorially.

His smile was as broad as the sun, which now fully engaged with the blue sky. Keeper had heard him singing the song all summer, practicing to sing those two words to Signe on this, the date of the blue moon, for this very day, this very night. It was right there on the calendar, the one that hung just above the driver's seat on the Bus.

How could she tell Dogie that everything was completely messed up?

Her legs started to itch. She felt an enormous need to go, to run and run and run and put the crabs and the roses behind her. Just past Dogie, past the ringing ukulele, past the breaking waves just in front of her, just offshore, she could see the sandbar, barely popping up above the water. De Vaca's Rock. The jammed-up apology made her feel nauseous. The Dr Pepper sloshed in her stomach.

She needed to tell Dogie now. About the crabs. And the gumbo. And everything. She opened her mouth to let the knot of words unravel. But just as she was about to blurt it all out, she heard a familiar voice: "C'mon, c'mon!" Captain, followed by BD and Too, bolted by, heading in the opposite direction. Without even thinking, she took off.

34

Dogie watched them go, the two dogs, the seagull, and the girl. He could tell that something was bothering Keeper by the way she had not looked up at him. He had never seen her stare at the ground for such a long time. Something was definitely on her mind.

He rolled his shoulders. She would tell him when she was ready. He knew what it was like to have a jumble of words get stuck in your mouth.

Dogie. He was not from Oyster Ridge Road. He wasn't even from Texas. In fact, he grew up in New Jersey. But right before he finished high school, a very convincing army recruiter had sat down with him at lunch, and as he tossed his four-cornered hat into the sky at the end of the graduation ceremony, before it fell back into his hand, he found himself in the army's boot camp. Three months later he was tramping through the hills of a distant country, packing a gun, teeth chattering, bombs exploding. By the time it was all over and he came home, back to New Jersey, he couldn't stop shaking. His hands shook. His knees shook. He couldn't eat or sleep. Even his head shook.

While he sat on his mother's sofa, he felt like he was going to rattle himself to pieces, like his bones would fly apart and scatter his body around the room if he didn't stop shaking. Finally, his mother sat down close to him one day on that sofa and simply wrapped her arms around him and told him that he was done now.

"Dogie," she said, "it's all right." And maybe it was her hugs. Maybe he just needed someone to say so. He wasn't sure. But all at once, the shaking stopped. Everything except his voice.

The doctor at the army hospital told him that he might stutter for the rest of his life, but he might not.

It didn't matter to Dogie. He could live with the

stutter, especially since the rest of him had stopped shaking.

Then he took all the money he had saved during the war and bought a big, yellow school bus. His mother told him, "Go find your true heart, honey." He had no idea where that could be, only that it wasn't in New Jersey. He hated to leave his mother, but he had to find a quiet place. He flipped a coin. "Heads, I'll g-g-go to the m-m-mountains. T-t-tails, I'll go to the sea." It was a shiny new quarter that he tossed into the air. When it smacked down into his broad palm, it was tails.

You might have thought that he'd go to the Jersey shore, but that was too busy for him. Or the rocky coast of California? But that water, he knew, was too cold. He wanted water he could wade into, even in the winter. So he pointed his bus toward Texas.

He drove for three days and three nights, and when he got to Houston, he turned south, not to Galveston, where he knew it would be like the Jersey shore, full of tourists, and not to Corpus Christi, same thing. Instead, he just ambled along until he got to a small place called Tater, which had only a handful of citizens and sat right at the entrance to a Texas state park. He drove past the gate, and while he drove, he eventually came to a road, or what looked like a road, made of oyster shells. Sure enough, it was Oyster Ridge Road, and even though the park was on either side, this particular road had been in private hands for nearly a hundred years. Three houses had stood there for generations.

One of them was the house in which Mr. Beauchamp lived. The other was newly taken over by the granddaughter of the original owner, along with her roommate. And the third belonged to a man in Tater who kept the place as a weekend fishing cottage but who lost his interest in fishing long ago. It was for rent.

Dogie signed the lease that day, then he got a permit from the Parks Department to open up a surfboard stand on the beach. He drove the yellow bus to the end of Oyster Ridge Road and parked it there, where it's stood for the past ten years, except for those days or nights when a storm blew in and he drove it to higher ground to keep it from washing away in the surf.

Every morning he rolled out the awning on the side of the Bus and got ready for the day. In fact, he was standing underneath the same awning when he laid eyes on Signe for the very first time.

Dogie remembered perfectly.

He was hanging up his bulletin board so that he could use it to tack up posters and T-shirts for sale, when a tall woman walked right by, her belly huge. She walked as fast as she could right into the surf, right into the waves, followed by a teenaged girl with shocking white hair calling, "Wait, wait! You can't do this here." But the taller one paid her no heed. They walked out past the shallow breakers, out to where the water was above their waists. He could see them bobbing in the waves.

Then Dogie heard them both start screaming. The two—one tall and dark; one shorter, with the whitest hair he'd ever seen.

At first Dogie dismissed their screams. Most

people screamed when they first went in the water, screamed at the cold, screamed at the first wave that splashed in their faces. Then he set down his hammer and listened. He could tell that these screams were different.

He recognized the scream from the taller one. A scream of pain.

The scream from the shorter one, a scream of fear.

War will let a person in to what a scream means.

Shaking off his flip-flops, he ran into the water, throwing himself in and swimming as fast as he could, their screams drowning out the roar of the tumbling waves.

And as he got nearer, he realized what had happened. There, in the arms of the shorter woman, a baby. And on the face of the taller one, tears.

Where was Meggie Marie now? he wondered. She could be anywhere, probably São Paulo or Singapore or San Francisco. Who knew?

He didn't miss Meggie Marie. This quiet place

along the coast had always been too small for her. He wasn't surprised when she left.

But he was grateful to her nonetheless. Grateful for two big reasons. First, she had brought Signe with her to Oyster Ridge Road. And second, she had given birth to Keeper.

Both of those reasons were significant.

Because of them, Dogie had found his true heart.

He strummed the ukulele and smiled. Then he sang his two-word song at the top of his lungs. Ten years. He'd waited ten years to sing this song for Signe, but he had loved her since the moment he met her.

35

Keeper was a fast runner. Her long legs powered her down the beach, but she was no match for the two dogs and the seagull. Soon enough, she pulled up and let them race ahead of her. She slowed down to a walk, her breath coming in large gulps. When she came directly in front of the sandbar, she paused and looked out.

A pair of brown pelicans perched on top of it. From where she stood, it looked like the two birds were standing on the water.

Anyone who has ever stood at the edge of a sandy beach, with the waves washing over his or her feet, knows the pull of the sea. Standing there, Keeper felt for the millionth time that firm tug, that beckoning pull from the water.

Keeper looked out at the sandbar. She had been out there before. She remembered the spray in her face, remembered how cold it felt. She could feel the sting of the salt in her eyes. It was the last place she had seen her mermaid mother.

But Keeper had not gone out there since. Signe had told her, "Don't ever do that again," and she hadn't. It was a solemn promise that she had made when she was three years old.

But that didn't keep her from wanting to go out there. From her spot on the beach, it looked so close. It looked like she could make it in just a few dozen strong strokes.

She took a step into the water, but as she did, the two pelicans lifted off of the sandbar and soared into the sky. Their raucous calls snapped her out of her reverie.

Her sneakers were soaking wet. Signe would be mad. *Madder!* Keeper turned away from the water. It was time to tell Dogie what had happened. She pulled her wet shoes off and gave them a shake. Then she crossed her fingers and hoped that Dogie would understand.

36

Dogie watched Keeper and the beasts come back toward him, first BD, then Too, and he stepped aside as Captain grabbed a wooden arm of his canvas deck chair.

"Easy th-th-th-there, b-b-b-birdman," said Dogie. Captain steadied himself on the arm of the chair and then fluffed his feathers up as if to say, *It's all good*. Dogie laughed and handed him a cheese cracker. Captain preferred watermelon, but cheese crackers were all Dogie had on hand at that particular moment. The bird snatched it out of his fingers.

Both of the dogs stretched out in the cool sand under the Bus, panting from their run. Dogie looked under there and could see their two pink tongues hanging out of their mouths. He filled a bowl with water from his Thermos and set it in the shade. "Yep, yep, yep!" barked Too, as if he approved.

"C'mon, c'mon!" The seagull fluffed his feathers again. Dogie held out another cheese cracker. Captain took it in his mouth, hopped onto the ground, and headed under the Bus to join the dogs.

From the corner of his eye, Dogie watched Keeper make her way toward the Bus. He was certain now, from the way she dragged her feet in the sand and held her head, that something was wrong. He picked up his ukulele, but then he set it down again on the chair, next to the box of cheese crackers, and walked toward Keeper. As he got closer, she looked right up at him, tall and thin, full of the wind and sun and sand and the whole beautiful day. Then suddenly, unexpectedly, with no warning at all, she ran into his arms and burst into an explosion of "sorry's." Dogie knelt down and wrapped his arms around her. So many "sorry's." He couldn't count them all.

37

Once Captain hopped underneath the Bus, he set his cheese cracker down on the sand in front of him and began to peck at it. As he did, the aroma of cheese cracker wafted into the noses of Too and BD.

"Yep, yep, yep!" yipped Too. He wanted a cheese cracker.

Mrrrurrrff, whined BD. He wanted a cheese cracker.

While Captain pecked, the two dogs stood up and began to sniff at Captain's cheese cracker. A dog's nose is tender. A seagull's beak is hard. Just as BD nudged his tender nose toward Captain's cheese cracker, *pop!* Captain pecked him, right in the most tender spot.

"Owwww!!!" BD howled.

And even though Too had stayed away from the fray, he also began to howl. All of this howling completely undid Captain. He hadn't meant to hurt BD. BD was, after all, his very best friend in the whole world.

And now what had he done? He had just pecked that same best friend on the most tender part of his nose and made him yelp! All because of a cheese cracker! Stupid cheese cracker. He didn't even like cheese crackers that much. Certainly not enough to hurt BD. He hadn't meant it. He wished he'd never even heard of cheese crackers! Cheese crackers. Bad.

But just as he was sinking into the lowest level of self-denouncement, he watched as BD grabbed the rest of the half-eaten cheese cracker and snarfed it right down. Wait! That was *his* cheese cracker! He started to peck BD again, but then he remembered.

Cheese crackers! He knew where there were plenty of cheese crackers. He hopped out from under the Bus. There on the chair, right where Dogie had set it, was the whole box. Cheese crackers for everyone!

"C'mon, c'mon!" he cried. He looked over his shoulder. He saw two dog noses poke out from under the Bus. "C'mon, c'mon!" He flapped his wings. Here they came. Tails wagging. Noses sniffing. Captain did a little hop on the arm of the chair. *Here they are*, he tried to say, pointing to the box on the chair.

BD's ears pointed forward. Too's ears pointed forward.

Ccchhhhheeeeeeessssseeee crrrrraaaaaccccckkkeeerssss!

Both of the dogs charged, right at the box of crackers. Captain hopped off the arm of the canvas deck chair just before the dogs hit it with all eight paws. *Crash! Crunch! Smash!* Chair and crackers went everywhere. "Yep, yep, yep!" Too ran around in circles, a cheese cracker hanging from his mouth. BD was munching away, his tail wagging like crazy.

Captain hopped up and down. "C'mon! c'mon!" he cried.

But there was another sound that he didn't notice. A sickening sound.

Sssnnnnnaaaapppp!

Dogie and Keeper walked up just in time to see Dogie's chair fold onto itself and crush the ukulele. A final ping from a snapped string emanated from under the canvas and wood.

Keeper stared in disbelief.

"Oh!" whispered Dogie as he pulled the ruined instrument out of the folds of the canvas chair. Keeper watched as Dogie picked up the broken ukulele and held it in both hands in front of him.

They both just stood there, not saying a single verb, noun, or even a syllable. And when Dogie finally tried to say something, to reassure her that it would be all right, the only thing he could say was, "It-it-it's okay, K-K-K-Keeper."

But Keeper knew it wasn't okay. In fact, she couldn't imagine anything ever being okay again.

And it was her fault. If she had told Dogie straight-away about the crabs and the bowl and the broken plants, none of this would have happened. Dogie would not have set his ukulele down on the chair, and he'd still be able to sing his song for Signe. She knew that he needed the ukulele to sing. For some reason, when he sang with his ukulele, his stutters disappeared.

How could Dogie sing at all now?

Keeper grabbed her finder dog by the collar and turned toward the haint blue house, the last thing in her ears Dogie's voice saying, "K-K-Keeper. It's ok-k-kay."

Except it wasn't. Not at all.

38

Now Keeper had to find Meggie Marie.
Somewhere in the universe.
Somewhere in the sea.

39

Speaking of the sea, an itty-bitty gnat of doubt buzzed by Keeper's head. Dogie had told Keeper that *The Scamper* was pondworthy, not exactly seaworthy.

"P-p-pondworthy," he had said after months and months of work.

Of course, she wasn't really planning to take it all the way out to sea, only to the sandbar, which, though it was technically in the sea, wasn't very far in the sea. See *Step I*, which does not say anything about the sea, only the sandbar.

Keeper stuck her thumb in her back pocket and felt the notebook paper, right there, her perfect plan.

Then she concentrated on the word "worthy." What difference did it make whether it was on the pond or in the sea, especially if the word "sea" was not in her plan? "Worthy" was enough. *The Scamper* was worthy.

Keeper had watched Dogie restore the boat from a battered old craft that someone had abandoned on the beach to the shiny red vessel she sat in now, had watched him sand the old wood until it felt like satin, then cover it with bright red paint—so many coats, she lost track.

Then one day she had tagged along behind him as he dragged it from the space underneath his house where he had worked on it, across the grass, and down to the Cut. Once there, he waited for her to climb aboard, then pushed them out onto the water.

Signe had not approved. Signe never approved when it came to being in or on the water. Signe was a lot like BD in that regard. "L-l-landlubbers," Dogie called them, with a chuckle.

Keeper had no idea who her real father was, but it didn't matter because Dogie had always been right next door. Dogie, who gave her new T-shirts all the time. Dogie, who kept the ancient green Dodge

station wagon running. Dogie, who played the ukulele for her and Signe every night after dinner and
who called her his "waxwing."

Dogie, who had been there when she was born.
As long as she had Dogie next door, Keeper did not
need a father. Nope. Dogie had
been there her whole entire life,
all ten years, every day. He even
had his own pet name for her:
"Good'un."

Dogie was like a bear, tall and broad shouldered, huge compared to Signe, who was wiry and compact, not much taller than Keeper now.

When Dogie invited Signe to come too, on that first lauching of *The Scamper*, she had crossed her arms and refused. "I'm perfectly glad to stay here," she'd said, pointing down to the ground. Keeper knew that Signe did not love the water like she and Dogie did. Keeper knew that Signe would never, ever climb aboard *The Scamper*. Not in a million years.

"We'll k-k-keep th-the boat here," Dogie had said, "here" meaning the Cut. "It's a p-p-perfect boat for this p-p-pond." Then he had added, "It's s-s-safe here."

The gnat of doubt buzzed a little louder in Keeper's ear. She waved her hand in the air to swat it away.

Later Dogie built the small pier that jutted down into the shallow water.

Signe's pier.

Whenever Keeper went out in the boat with Dogie, Signe would take her yellow deck chair to the end of the pier and sit. She always wore a life vest.

"Somebody has to be the lifeguard," she told them. Keeper and Dogie thought that was hilarious. They knew that if Signe ever got in the water, someone would likely have to rescue *her*, not the other way around. "I've been in the water twice," she reminded them, not joining in the hilarity. "And I'm still here, aren't I?"

The first time Signe had gone into the water was on the day Keeper was born. It was not in the pond; rather, it was in the surf, right in the Gulf of Mexico. Signe had told Keeper about that day so many times, Keeper could almost picture it. "Yep, that was my first swim," Signe told her. Then she added, "Yours too, Sweet Pea."

Signe never talked about her second swim. "Twice is enough" is all she would say.

But Keeper didn't think too hard about Signe swimming. Instead, she had concentrated on learning about the boat.

Out there, Dogie had shown her how to use the oars to steer, how to lean on either side to get the boat to respond to her. It was a fine little boat. She loved the way it rode just on top of the water, but low enough to see a few inches down, to see the sparkling sun perch that made their home there, and on mornings when she got up early enough, she might catch a glimpse of the stingrays when they slipped in on the high tide.

Keeper thought stingrays were beautiful, flying through the water, their wide wings rippling like echoes of the currents. They looked like angels. Water angels. She had never seen a real angel, but she imagined that they might look like the gray-brown stingrays that slid beneath *The Scamper*.

They were most definitely cooleoleo.

"J-j-just beware of their tails," cautioned Dogie. She knew all about their barbed tails, but when she saw them, just beneath the water's surface, she still thought of angels.

Then Dogie added another caution, but this one had nothing to do with the stingrays. "D-d-don't ever get t-t-too close . . ." He didn't finish his sentence, just pointed to the narrow ditch that cut between the sand dunes, allowing the water from the tides to run back and forth, filling up and emptying the pond. That's why it was called "the Cut."

Keeper knew that if she got very near the ditch when the moon pulled the tide back, it would take her right out with it, right out into the sea.

Tonight she was counting on it. *Step H.*

Keeper looked up. There it was, the very thinnest top of the moon, peeking out of an almost invisible bank of clouds.

"It's about time!" she told it. And as if the moon had heard her loud and clear, it sent another rolling wave underneath the boat and lifted it just below the edge of the pier, knocking against it with a resounding thud. The rope hung down as loose as could be.

It was a sign. Time. To. Go. And with that, Keeper gave a good, hard tug on the loosened knot that held the boat to the pier.

Step F. Check!

F for "free"!

They were free, free, free! And as if *The Scamper* were majorly happy to finally be cut loose from the dock, she trembled from nose to stern. Open water! Keeper stood right up and did a little happy boat dance, right there under the rising moon.

But instead of heading toward the channel like Keeper had planned, *The Scamper* yawed and lurched in the opposite direction, right toward the salt grass marsh, the exact place Keeper didn't want to go.

10

"Noooooo!!!!" Keeper shouted. "No no no no no!"

She was *not* going to go in the wrong direction, not after all this waiting, no way, no how, no-siree-bob. She was *not* going to get stuck in that mucky marsh full of giant snapping turtles, and not just *any* snapping turtles, but alligator snapping turtles. *Uh-uh!* Pass the beans and stir the corn, there was no way she was going to let her boat—Dogie's boat—float into that swamp, and then she'd for sure have to call for help, which would mean she'd be in even deeper trouble than she already was.

"No no no no no no!" she said again.

She sat back down fast, snatched up the oars, jammed them in the oarlocks, and started rowing, which wasn't as easy as it had seemed when Dogie was the one doing the rowing. She pulled extra hard on her left oar to turn the boat around, but the incoming tide, the one she had waited and waited and waited for, seemed to be rolling in with gusto now.

She had untied the boat too soon. She had not waited long enough for the tide to finish rising. How could she have forgotten? It was right there in *Step F*.

Too late.

No matter how hard she pulled, *The Scamper* would not turn around.

"Grrrr..." She gritted her teeth. "Turn!" she yelled, but the nose of the boat refused to come around.

As she leaned back and dug into the water, she swore she could hear the *snicker-snack* of the snapping turtles just waiting for her to float right into their snapping jaws.

41

From his nest in the sabal palm tree, Captain woke up from his seagull sleep. He had an itch just behind his head. With his eyes still closed, he fluffed up his feathers and scratched the itch with his foot. He settled back in and waited to fall back to sleep.

But the itch did not go away. Uh-oh. Not a good sign.

He opened his eyes. Captain was a deep sleeper. With the exception of a storm, only a couple of things ever woke him up in the middle of the night. An itch or a worry.

With an itch, he could scratch it and then fall back to sleep. With a worry, no matter how much he scratched, it wouldn't go away.

Tonight the itch could not be scratched. What he had was a worry.

But where was it coming from?

He looked toward the dark house. It was all buttoned up, the same as every night.

He glanced across the road and saw Mr. Beauchamp and Sinbad sitting on their porch. He noticed that Dogie and Too's house, like usual, was dark and quiet. He scanned the night sky. There was the moon, right where it should be. Everything appeared to be the same as usual.

Still, he couldn't shake the feeling that something wasn't right. Then the worry became a question: Was BD in trouble? The worry itched like crazy. He stood up in his nest and shook his head. He listened. But he didn't hear BD's voice. If the dog needed him, he'd howl for him, yes?

He leaned into the damp air.

Nothing.

He fluffed his feathers again, then stretched his wings. He spread his good wing out over the edge of the nest as far as he could. He used the pinfeathers on his wing tip to test the wind velocity.

Sssssssstttttttrrrrrrreeeeettttcccchhhh!!!!

Then he did the same with his bent wing. *Ouch!* There was always a small achy pinch in that wing. He flapped it a couple of times to shake out the ouch. He looked around some more. His stomach growled.

Ahhh, he thought, *maybe I'm just hungry.*

It's a fact that seagulls are always hungry. They are basically hungry twenty-four hours a day. Even when they are asleep, they are hungry. A seagull is an eating machine. Captain was no exception.

He pulled his wings back in and admired the way the moonbeams settled on his bright white feathers and how they made his black feathers gleam. He was a study in black and white. But he didn't dwell on his appearance since what he really wanted to concentrate on, now that he had established that the worry was just a figment of his imagination . . . maybe . . . was his empty stomach.

Since the moon was full, he figured that the little minnows in the Cut would be near the surface of the water, a good time to skim over the pond and pluck up a few. Minnows would be a perfect night-time snack. Thinking about them made him fluff up his feathers again.

He hopped onto the edge of the nest. Due to his bent wing, takeoffs and landings were not his strong suit. He had to chart his flight plan in advance to compensate for the crooked wing. Instead of flying straight ahead, he tended to list a little to the left. So he flew in wide semicircles. It took him a little longer than other seagulls to arrive at his destination, but he did usually manage to make it . . . eventually.

He scanned the pond. The beams from the moon sparkled on the water's surface. Yep, he could practically taste those salty little minnows. Just a quick scoop, and he'd be back in time to sleep some more until breakfast. Ahhh, minnows. Just the thing.

He took a deep breath and . . . hop . . . into the sky he flew. He tilted a little to the left, then a little to the right until he gained his balance. Then down, down, down he went, toward the water's surface. But just as he made his last semicircle, he swooped up short.

There was something floating on the pond. Some*one* floating on the pond. No. Wait. There were *two* some-ones floating on the pond.

He flew closer. It was Keeper! And BD!! They were out too. Just like he was! Oh, happy day, calloo callay!

"C'mon, c'mon!" he cried. It could be minnows for everyone!

42

Down below, Keeper pulled on her oars. With *The Scamper*'s flat bottom, if she didn't get it turned around, she'd get stuck when the tide fell, held fast by the saw-toothed grass and the thick, silty muck.

A girl doesn't grow up on the edge of a salt grass swamp without hearing about the denizens of that same swamp. Not only were there a gazillion snakes and cooters, but the worst were the alligator snapping turtles. And even though she had never had a close encounter with any of them, she knew about them nonetheless.

She'd seen their gnarly beaks and their sawback shells. She knew that if one grabbed on to one of her toes or a finger, it could bite it clean off. Thinking about it made her curl her toes up inside her sneakers.

And what about BD's toes?

"No toes!" she yelled. She was not going to sacrifice any of their toes to those stupid turtles. Not one single toe!

She tugged on the oars as hard as she could, but the boat still drifted toward the looming banks. As if the tide were playing a trick on her, another wave rolled up beneath her and pushed her farther forward.

Swoosh!

The boat felt like it was flying toward the marsh. Keeper dug her right oar into the water and, with her left, paddled paddled paddled. Dip dip dip.

"Turrrnnnnn," she called to the boat. She pulled back as hard as she could.

Every muscle in her body felt as taut as the strings on Dogie's ukulele.

"Turrrnnnnn," she called again. She clenched her teeth. She was *not not not not not* going to float into that stupid marsh with those stupid turtles. She dug her oars into the water and *puuuullllledddd.*

Then . . .

    slowly . . .

      slowly . . .

        slowly . . . the breeze sat down,

          the tide paused and at last! . . .

the boat turned its nose away from the marsh. Finally, she headed toward the opposite shore, toward the ditch on the far side of the pond. "Yes!" she cried. They were moving forward now, straight toward the channel that would take them out to sea.

"Yeehaw!" she whooped.

She stashed the oars, then, one at a time, she flexed her surfboard-waxing muscles. *Hooray*, she thought, *for all that waxing.*

A wave of happy rolled over Keeper. But only for a second, for as they floated toward the ditch, they passed the small pier, Signe's pier, nestled in the shadows. Keeper glanced toward it. The emptiness of it startled her. It was too empty. Signe was not sitting there on her yellow deck chair, watching. Being the lifeguard.

Suddenly, a small memory bubbled through Keeper: Signe reaching for her, pulling her out of the water, pulling her out of some other boat, a long time ago. Signe holding on to her, holding her tight, both of them sopping wet, drenched.

"Just you and me, Sweet Pea"—Signe's words in her ears, the last thing she heard every night.

The empty pier grew smaller as she drifted away from it. Keeper looked beyond the pier at her house, also growing smaller. She knew that, inside, Signe was fast asleep in the room next to hers. Without even thinking, Keeper reached out toward her fading house, where Signe slept, as if she might tap Signe on the shoulder and wake her up and say, *Here I am!* But then she felt her mother's charm bump against her chest. She looked down at it, aglow in the moon's dim light.

"Pull," she told the moon, "pull."

43

With the moon on the rise, Keeper picked up the oars again. *Ouch!* She dropped them quickly, shaking her hands one at a time. Wow! Her hands felt like a dozen bees had stung them. Dogie hadn't told her that rowing would hurt her hands so much! Both of them felt raw from pulling on the oars.

When she had first started her waxwing job, she had gotten some blisters from the comb that she used to remove the old wax, but she didn't remember her hands feeling this achy. She shook them again.

She made a mental note about adjusting *Step G*, part of which stated: *row across the pond toward the channel.* Instead, she changed it to: *float across the pond toward the channel.* That way, she could give her hands a rest before they hit the open water, where she knew she'd have to row again. So she stowed the oars under the seat and let the boat drift.

Anyway, for now, the water was pulling her in the exact right direction. Exactly! Then she remembered. "Time to give Yemaya a gift," she told BD.

Mr. Beauchamp had told her that Yemaya was the big mama. But he had also told her that Yemaya was unreliable. "If she doesn't like her gift, she might brew up a storm, maybe a hurricane, maybe a tidal wave." Then he paused and added, "She *might* grant a wish, but she always expects a gift."

Now Keeper reached into her shoe box and pulled out one of her merlings. She held it between her thumb and fingers, so small, the roundness of it soft to her touch, then she lifted it close to her face so that she could see it more clearly in the dark.

"Ohhh. Sedna," she said. She rubbed the carving's boxy hands, the fur collar and round face. She felt a small twinge in her throat, then swallowed it down.

"Sedna," she began. She swallowed again, then went

on, "I'm sorry that you're so far from home." Sedna was the ancient sea goddess of the Arctic, one of the most famous, most revered of all of the merrow.

Keeper had discovered Sedna in a piece of spruce that had been tossed on the beach after a winter storm a few years ago. She remembered that the wet spruce felt almost silky to her touch. The little carving still felt that way. Silky.

"I'll miss you," she whispered.

She looked out across the darkness, so thick and deep. "Yemaya," she called, "big mama of all the oceans, a gift for you." Then, before she could change her mind, she threw the tiny figure of Sedna into the brackish water of the pond.

Plunk! Keeper heard it splash, and when she did, she closed her eyes. Sedna was one of her favorites, and she didn't think that after today Mr. Beauchamp would ever carve her another.

Thinking about Mr. Beauchamp carving the merlings reminded her of the piece of juniper she had only recently found and presented to him. The

juniper was still sitting on his side table, right next to his carving knife. She knew exactly which of the merrow was supposed to be made from it, and she had told Mr. Beauchamp, but so far he had not started the carving. And now he was so mad at her, she doubted that he ever would.

She looked inside the box at the five merlings still there, still nestled atop the soft purple T-shirt. She patted the one in her pocket. BD whined.

And just over her head, the familiar call of Captain. "C'mon, c'mon."

44

The only thing Captain ever said was, "C'mon, c'mon!"

Of course, anyone who has ever listened closely to seagulls knows that is their common language. Regardless of port or river or even inland lake, "c'mon, c'mon" is the lexicon of seagulls.

A few humans understand this. Shrimp boat sailors, for example, know that when a seagull sings, "C'mon, c'mon," it means, *Come on, throw me a shrimp.* That is why there are always seagulls trailing behind shrimp boats. The shrimpers understand seagull talk.

Small children on the beach also know this language. Seagulls love this about tiny humans. They, the seagulls, love to fly just in front of them and play chase. "C'mon, c'mon," say the seagulls, and soon enough, those little shorties start running.

Early on, while his wing was still mending, Captain taught the people in the haint blue house the meaning behind "c'mon, c'mon." Now, every morning, he flew onto the porch from his nest in the palm orchard, and he said it loud and clear right outside the kitchen door. This was usually followed by Keeper letting him in, which was then followed by something tasty coming Captain's way, maybe a chunk of cantaloupe or a cracker.

If he said it again, "C'mon, c'mon," Keeper would sometimes hand over something else, a strawberry or a potato chip or even his favorite, his most beloved, his all-time highest exalted sublime most delicious stultifyingly extremely wonderful marvelous fantastic yes yes yes: watermelon!

Captain loved watermelon.

Yep. He would do just about anything for a big, juicy chunk of watermelon. Anything, anything, anything.

In fact, it was because of watermelon that he could fly at all. After he seemed healed from the accident with the kitchen window, Keeper had tucked him under her arm and carried him down the porch stairs and set him in the yard. Signe had stayed upstairs on the porch and lined the porch rail with cubes of ripe, red watermelon. It was roughly twelve feet from the ground to the porch rail. From his spot in the yard, Captain could see the brilliant crimson cubes all in a row. He could smell them, juicy and sweet, luscious.

He called out, "C'mon, c'mon," which meant, *C'mon, throw that watermelon this way.* But instead of following his orders, Signe turned around and went back inside. Keeper knelt down and whispered to him, "Watermelon, Captain." Then she stroked his back and gently pulled both of his wings out to his sides and said this one thing: "Fly!" And before he could worry about the ache in his mended wing, before he could even think about it, he lifted himself off the ground and flew.

It wasn't pretty. It wasn't straight. But he did, in fact, fly. And he also ate a lot of watermelon.

So now, whenever someone said, "Watermelon,

Captain," he'd head right for the porch of the haint blue house. And almost always, there'd be a juicy red chunk right there, waiting for him.

But now here was his girl. Here was his dog. Right out here in the open. Not on the porch, but in the small boat on the pond. He lined them up in his sights and shifted his weight into landing mode. "C'mon, c'mon," he cried.

And with a swoop, down he went.

45

Keeper ducked just in time to avoid being clipped by a bundle of white and black feathers. She covered her face while Captain dropped clumsily on top of BD, who gave a yelp.

BD was used to Captain using him as a landing and launching pad, but he still complained. Nevertheless, he couldn't deny that he was happy to see the bird. In the moon's bright light, Keeper could see BD's happy expression.

And she could hear the sound from the waves getting louder and louder. They were getting closer! All at once, an invisible spider of worry crawled up her spine. If she did it now, she thought, she could still turn around. There was still time.

She pulled the life vest tight against her chest. Its canvas cloth was scratchy under her bare arms.

She looked at BD again, the seagull perched atop him. The worry spider skittered down her back. Was it fair to take a landlubber dog out to sea? In the middle of the night?

BD nudged her arm with his wet nose and licked the skin under her wrist. She wiped it against the rough cloth of the life vest. Then a new thought occurred to her. How could she not have had this thought before? "You need a life vest!" she told him.

As if he understood her, he shook his head so hard, his ears flapped against the sides of his mouth. She leaned back to keep the slobber from spraying her face.

Why, no, he seemed to say.

"Why, yes," she replied, "you do." And with that, she pulled the other life vest, Dogie's, out from under the bench. "If I have to wear one, you do too."

Unlike her own yellow vest, Dogie's was bright orange and about twice as large. She lifted BD's front paws one at a time and slipped them into the

armholes of the vest, then pulled the straps as tight as she could. The pulling hurt her hands, but she pulled anyway, and in a few moments he was fully invested. "There," she said.

BD whined unhappily. Then he tried to shake the big vest off. It was way too big on him, and it hung down between his legs when he stood up. But it wasn't coming off. Keeper could see that.

"Sit down," she said, and when he did, the back of it popped up behind his head.

She couldn't help it, the sight of him made her laugh. "You look like you're wearing a pup tent," she said, admiring her own joke. Then she added, "If I have to be careful, so do you." BD did not seem convinced; he plopped down in the bottom of the boat, right at her feet, and sighed. Captain hopped down on top of him and settled in.

The life vest around BD made Keeper feel even better. Her worry spider disappeared, at least for now.

46

As the boat slowly skimmed the top of the pond, Keeper felt the soft rocking motion of it through her feet, her legs, all the way up her body. For a moment she felt fastened to the world unto itself, the sturdy wood of the boat beneath her, the winking stars above her. All at once, she thought she heard her name again.

Keeper. Keeper.

Then she remembered an old song that her mother used to sing to her.

You are my little mergirl—there it was, Meggie Marie's chiming voice in her ear.

And I'm your mermaid mama.

Yes, an old nursery rhyme, one of the few things she remembered from her mother:

Swim, my little water sprite
From Zealand to Bahama
You are my little mergirl
And I'm your mermaid mama.

The rhyme rang through her head. It all felt so familiar. The boat and the water and her mother's voice, the deep, deep darkness.

Then a question blew in on the breeze: *Where is Signe?* Keeper scratched her arm where another mosquito had just taken a bite. Signe was asleep, of course. In the haint blue house.

47

The haint blue house. Painted that way by its current resident, Signe. "To keep the ghosts at bay," she had joked.

Before that, it had been as gray as a stormy sky, made so by years of blowing sand, which erased all the original paint. No one even knew what the first color had been. "Blowing sand will do that to paint," Signe had said.

Haints. Signe had never even heard that word until she moved south. Maybe they could be found in Iowa, the place she grew up, maybe not. She had never believed in ghosts anyway, so what did it matter?

The old house needed a fresh coat of paint. That was all. At least on the outside. Inside, the house was exactly the way Meggie Marie's grandmother had left it. The cupboards held her white dishes with the blue morning glories on the rims. The walls were lined with shelves that held volumes and volumes of old books, mostly books by Victorian authors, but also an occasional travelogue, which had confused Signe since Mr. Beauchamp told her that Keeper's great-grandmother never traveled anywhere but to Tater and back.

The old woman did not have many clothes, but what she had was still hanging in the backs of closets, pushed back to make room for Signe's and Keeper's things. And Meggie Marie's. There were still some things of hers in the backs of the closets too.

Sometimes, when Signe managed to get a day off from her job at the Prince Oyster Bar and Bar, she took one of the abandoned skirts or blouses or pair of shoes to the Tater Thrift Shop, to exchange it for something for Keeper. After all, a growing girl needs clothes.

In the bathroom there were soft white cotton towels on the shelves and even softer white cotton sheets for the beds. There were seashells and starfish in the windowsills and yellow curtains in the windows themselves. And everything was tidy and clean.

When Keeper had asked, "Will the paint really keep the haints away?" Signe had shrugged and answered with her stock reply: "That is a question for the universe."

When Keeper was born, Signe was only fifteen. Three years later, when Signe was eighteen, that's when Meggie Marie disappeared.

And not too long after that, Signe painted the house haint blue.

48

Keeper noticed that the wind was picking up. BD and Captain were curled into a ball at her feet. They didn't seem one bit excited about slipping into the channel.

How could they sleep at a time like this? But neither of them budged. Not an inch to the east. Not an inch to the west.

Couple of lazybones, she thought. *They'll miss the ride through the Cut at this rate!* Which made her think that it was time for another offering.

She reached into her shoe box and pulled out another merling.

"Hello, *ningyo*," she said, in a voice so soft, only the tiny figure could hear. She knew which one it was without looking, thanks to the tooth marks on either side of its body, put there by BD last spring.

That day after school, Keeper had run into her bedroom, taken the merlings out of her backpack, and stuffed them down into her jeans pocket, then headed out, out to the Bus. There Dogie had a cold Dr Pepper waiting for her, just like he always did.

Keeper took the merlings out of her pocket and lined them up in the sand. Then, while BD and Too snoozed, and Dogie drew in his sketchbook, she built sand cottages for her carvings.

Too soon, Dogie told her it was closing time. She scooped up the merlings, put them in her pocket, and helped Dogie fold up the beach umbrellas and chairs and stow them in the Bus.

When Keeper got home, she took the merlings out of her pocket and lined them up on her dresser, just like she did every day. "One, two, three, four, five, six . . ." She gasped. There were only six.

She counted them over and over. One was missing. She knew which one at once.

"The *ningyo!*" She dug her hand deeper into her pocket. Nothing.

She started to retrace her steps back to the Bus, but it was already dark outside. "No way, missy," said Signe, when Keeper told her she was going back out. "You'll have to wait until you get home from school tomorrow."

Keeper stomped her foot. "But —"

Signe cleared her throat. Foot stomping was not allowed in the haint blue house. Keeper went back to her bedroom. The six remaining merlings seemed to be staring at her. She turned them around so that she couldn't see their accusing faces.

What could she say to them? She didn't have any words to offer up to the remaining figurines. That night she had a hard time sleeping. The *ningyo!* How could she have lost him?

But then, when she woke up the next morning, there, standing by her bed, his tail wagging at a furious clip, BD dropped something on the pillow next to her face.

The *ningyo!* She hugged BD and then ran to tell Signe the good news. It wasn't until she set the little merling on the top of the dresser with the others, which she turned face out again, that she noticed the tooth marks.

"Grrrr . . . ," she growled at BD.

"Grrrr . . . ," he growled back. And she burst into laughter.

The damage didn't matter at all to her; she still loved the beautiful carving. In fact, the scars made him somehow more real to her, proof of his realness. She did not say this to Signe.

Now she held the *ningyo* in the flat of her palm. She chewed on the inside of her mouth. She had lost him once before, and now she would lose him for good.

The *ningyo* was almost entirely fish. He had no arms or chest or waist. Only his face was human. He had a long, single-strand mustache that hung down on either side of his mouth like the trailing whiskers of a catfish. To Keeper, he always looked solemn, as if he were grimacing at the tooth marks left in his lovely scales.

Ningyo, all the way from Japan. Mr. Beauchamp had told her that fishermen sometimes caught these merfolk in their nets and ate them and that their flesh was supposed to be delicious. He also told her that anyone who ate a *ningyo* would live for a thousand years. "Older than barnacles," he said.

Keeper rolled the tiny figure between her fingers one last time, memorizing the tooth marks. She looked at BD and smiled. Maybe BD would live for a thousand years because he had taken a bite out of the *ningyo*. It was a thought that made her happy.

She held the *ningyo* up so that they were eye to eye. "Go back to the sea," she told him. And with that, she lowered the figure into the water beside her boat. She thought she would not miss the *ningyo* as much as she missed Sedna. But she was wrong.

For a brief moment she could see him floating on top of the waves, and then he was gone. "Yemaya," she called out, "here's another gift for you." The water beneath *The Scamper* pulled her faster.

Keeper closed the lid of the shoe box. There were

only five more figurines left. Only five. Four in the box. And one in her pocket.

And maybe, thought Keeper, *if my perfect plan keeps working, Mr. Beauchamp will carve that juniper.*

"Onward with *Step G!*" she announced.

49

Ashore in the haint blue house, Signe slept, unaware that Keeper was gone, slowly drifting toward the sea with BD and Captain.

When she had finally fallen into bed, exhausted from the long day, she welcomed the solace of sleep, like a flying carpet that carried her away from the terrible day, especially from Keeper's inexplicable behavior.

Even in her dreams, however, Signe kept replaying her argument with Keeper. There she was, standing in the doorway of Keeper's room and yelling, "What in the world were you thinking?" And then Keeper kept saying something about the crabs and how they were talking to her.

Of all things—crabs!

The crabs that Dogie had caught. The ones he had

gotten up before sunrise to catch. Those crabs. The ones she was supposed to add to her gumbo.

And on top of the crabs, what about her bowl? What about Mr. Beauchamp's flowers? What about Dogie?

"Are you telling me that all of this happened because of *crabs*?" Signe had demanded. She felt the hair on her arms rise with her growing anger.

Here was Keeper, right in front of her, almost as tall as she was, growing up before her very eyes, her chin jutting out in the same way that Meggie Marie's used to jut out, especially when she was about to deliver a big, fat lie.

So many times Meggie Marie had told Signe that she was just going into town to pick up something from the store, and then she wouldn't return for hours, leaving her and Keeper alone without even a car. And what about the times Meggie Marie had told Signe that she would pick her up from work at the Prince Oyster Bar and Bar but then "forget." More than once, Signe had found herself walking home or calling Dogie to come get her.

Meggie Marie had told a lot of lies.

To Signe's knowledge, Keeper had never lied to her before, but Meggie Marie certainly had. And now here was Keeper with that same jutting-out chin.

"They talked to me," Keeper insisted.

"Talking crabs?!" shouted Signe. "Keeper, crabs can't talk."

Keeper jutted her chin out farther. "But I'm part mermaid." As if that explained everything.

"Aaaargghh!" yelled Signe. She couldn't even seem to form a distinct word. Mermaids! Fury like she hadn't felt for seven years zipped through her chest, her arms, the top of her head. She felt like every nerve, every muscle, every tendon might snap at the smallest movement.

"Keeper!" she finally yelled, out of pure frustration, but any other words that she might have said stuck in her throat and refused to come out. The only thing left to do was slam the door. *WHAM!*

If there were any haints about, they surely skedaddled.

• • •

Signe had tried so hard to do everything right when it came to raising Keeper, to make sure that she was safe, to teach her the things she needed to know, to show her how to care for the world unto itself and its denizens. But today she felt like the worst mother in the universe. All this time, she'd let her girl believe in something that wasn't true.

Then Signe knew: It was time to tell Keeper that there was no such thing as magic or mermaids or talking crabs. A girl who is ten years old should know the truth.

"Keeper," Signe whispered in her sleep. She had no idea that her girl was drifting away.

50

For Signe, this was not the way this night was supposed to turn out. That morning she had risen early, before the sun. The moon, left over from the night before, not quite full, but almost, still hung in the western sky just above the Cut. She glanced at it and toasted it with her cup of coffee. "Blue moon tonight," she said happily.

Right after Meggie Marie had left—in fact, only days later—Signe had gone to the Tater Public Library and checked out every book she could find on raising children. One of them, she couldn't remember which one, had talked about the importance of family traditions.

"Family traditions," she remembered saying. Then she had closed the book and wondered what kind of family traditions she could create without a traditional family. But then she found the old cookbook at the Tater Friends of the Library Book Sale, the one that had a recipe for "Blue Moon Gumbo."

For best results, make on the day of the blue moon. Invite your family. That's what the recipe said.

So that's what Signe had done. Once or twice a year, whenever the moon was blue, she made a huge pot of crab gumbo and invited her "family," all of the residents of Oyster Ridge Road—only two besides herself and Keeper—and made blue moon gumbo. And *bingo!* She had a tradition.

And just that morning, coffee cup in hand, recipe open in front of her, she could hardly wait for the evening to come. She had looked back out through the window at Dogie's house. The light was on in his kitchen too. Dogie, she was sure, was already at the beach, seining for crabs. She had told him the night before, "If you'll catch the crabs, I'll cook the gumbo." And he had smiled at her. Dogie loved her gumbo. Soon he would walk through the door with a tub full of snapping crabs, fresh from the Gulf of Mexico.

The pages in the old cookbook were ragged and torn, which meant that the recipes had been used and used some more, a sure sign of wonderful food. The cookbook had not disappointed, and Signe's gumbo recipe always tasted amazingly wonderful, spicy and rich. *Yummm!*

Signe loved these gumbo nights. She loved sitting around the table in her kitchen with the people she cared about most of all right there—Dogie, Keeper, and Mr. Beauchamp. All of them.

She loved that she had made a tradition all their own. Blue moon gumbo.

She closed her eyes and imagined the way the night would go. All of them, Dogie, Signe, Mr. Beauchamp, and Keeper, along with the assortment of beasts— Dogie's little dog, Too; BD and Captain; Sinbad— would eat gumbo until their stomachs were full. Of course, there would be watermelon for Captain.

Then Dogie would take out his ukulele and sing as

many songs as he could think of with the word "moon" in them. That was a lot of songs. Some of them she would know and would sing along with. Keeper would dance and twirl, her girl, her tall and lanky twirling girl. Mr. Beauchamp would fall asleep in his chair, and they would have to help him back to his house and wait for him to settle into his porch chair. Sinbad would weave in and out between their legs and finally jump into the old sailor's lap before drifting off too.

And after a while Keeper's eyes would get so heavy, she wouldn't be able to stay awake any longer, and Signe would tuck her into bed, with BD nestled on the rug next to her.

And then, at last, she and Dogie would sit outside on the porch that wrapped itself all around the haint blue house. Signe would smoke her cigarette, the one she allowed herself each night, even though she knew it was bad for her, and Dogie would play his ukulele, only he wouldn't sing any more songs, just run his fingers over the nylon strings.

And meanwhile, across the road, Mr. Beauchamp,

sitting on his own porch, would wait and wait and wait until the moon was right at the top of the sky, when his night-blooming cyrus, the queens of the night, would burst into bloom. He had waited all summer, all year, for the gigantic flowers to open. And tonight, the night of the blue moon, this would be the night. Even though he would be snoozing, Signe knew that he would wake up in time for the blossoms to open. He always did.

Then the heavy aroma from the huge flowers would waft across Oyster Ridge Road and encircle them all.

A tradition. That's what her blue moon gumbo was. But there was one more item that the recipe called for: a wish. Right there, at the bottom of the list of ingredients, the recipe said, *Stir in one wish.*

Always before, Signe had stirred in wishes for things like good health for Keeper, big tips from her customers at the Prince Oyster Bar and Bar, and decent tires for the green Dodge station wagon. But not tonight. Tonight she would wish for Dogie to sing his two-word song for her. While he and Keeper thought they were keeping it a secret, she had heard him practicing it when she had walked down to the Bus to pick up Keeper after work one day.

She had been waiting for him to sing this song for her for ten years. And finally, tonight while Keeper slept and Mr. Beauchamp watched his beautiful cyrus blooms greet the moon, maybe, if she wished hard enough, he would sing it just for her, and she, in turn, would tell him how much she loved him, how much she had always loved him. That had been the plan.

But now, that cold round moon rising in the eastern sky, nothing had gone according to plan, nothing. No gumbo. No twirling girl. No blossoms of the night. And no ukulele, either.

Now here was Signe, wrung out from the day left behind, unaware that her girl was all alone, with only her dog and a bent-winged seagull for company. Alone and drifting away.

Wake up, Signe. Wake up.

51

It seems like a girl should know about her very own mother, doesn't it? Once, a long time ago, Keeper had asked Signe, "Did my mama love me?" and without even a small hesitation, Signe had answered, "Yes, Keeper. Oh, yes."

But then Keeper asked another question: "Did we love her?"

This time Signe paused. Keeper felt the time stretch out like the next-to-last day of school, the longest day of the year. The pause seemed like that. But then Signe looked right at Keeper and said, "We loved her, Sweet Pea. We did."

The thing is, Keeper did not remember that. She did not remember loving Meggie Marie. She only remembered waiting for her. Are loving and waiting the same thing? Keeper had wondered this many times. It was a question for the universe.

But the big question right now was could she manage to get her little vessel to come aground atop De Vaca's Rock?

So far, in the perfect plan, she had checked off *Steps A, B, C, D, E,* and *F.* Amended *Step G* was in progress. She was now on the cusp of *Step H: Go through the channel.* And then she would embark upon *Step I: Row to the sandbar.*

Keeper knew what she needed to do: point *The Scamper's* prow directly into the waves and steer it straight toward the rock. Surfers always avoided it because it scraped their boards. But she was going to make a beeline for it. Straight ahead, mateys! All hands on deck!

But just then Keeper had a disturbing thought: Would the sandbar leave a ding in *The Scamper*?

Dings in surfboards were a problem. Then again, surfboards were made out of fiberglass. *The Scamper* was made of much sturdier wood. Keeper gingerly patted both sides of the boat with her sore hands.

Yep, the wood was as solid as could be, not at all like those flimsy-whimsy surfboards with their thin fiberglass skins. She decided: No need to worry about dings. Nope.

Keeper rubbed the charm around her neck. And then she said to BD and Captain, "I can make a wish on the charm, can't I?" When a girl is ten, she is full to the brim with wishes. Wishes on stars, wishes on tooth fairies, wishes on fishes. A lucky charm should be chock-full of wishes, shouldn't it?

Right there Keeper made a majorly big wish: "Make everything all right," she said. And then, so she wouldn't make Yemaya feel left out, she called out again to the great mother of the sea, "Help me find my mother."

It was a boatload of wishing.

And to seal the deal, she opened the shoe box and lifted out another figurine. The siren. She could tell by its sharp shoulder blades. "Those are what's left of her wings," Mr. Beauchamp had explained.

Quickly, before she could change her mind, she set

the siren into the water and turned her head. She couldn't watch, but after all those wishes, she felt good.

"We can do this," she said to BD and Captain. "Easy peasy!"

52

There are many stories of sirens. Some have a split tail like the Sheila-na-gig of Ireland. Some look like movie stars and have no tail at all. But Keeper's siren was from an older tribe. As the story goes, there is an enchanted island somewhere in the Greek Isles that was home to the beautiful Cyrenes, winged women whose songs were so lovely that sailors could not resist them and drove their boats onto the rocky cliffs that protected the shores. These were the creatures Odysseus encountered on his long quest.

But through the years, their name was changed to "sirens" and their bodies were changed from birds to fish.

Maybe it was a siren, and not a regular ol' mermaid, who had lured Cabeza de Vaca onto the sandbar off of Oyster Ridge Road five hundred years ago. A siren and her song.

53

Speaking of songs, here was a question that Keeper had asked over and over: How was it that whenever Dogie played his ukulele and sang along with it, he never ever stuttered? Instead, the words were always crystal clear. There were so many questions for the universe.

54

Signe, fast asleep, not knowing that her girl was out in *The Scamper*, knew that what she had said was true, that she had loved Meggie Marie. Loved her like a sister.

In the small den of the haint blue house, she kept a framed photo of Meggie Marie on the sofa table, an old black-and-white shot cut out of the *Galveston Daily News*, with the caption, "Mermaid Queen Leads Parade." The photograph was fuzzy and yellowed, but it showed Meggie Marie atop a float shaped like a giant nautilus shell, her mermaid crown atop her head, her smile as wide as the ocean itself, a smile so much like Keeper's.

Yes. Signe had loved Meggie Marie. But she did not miss her.

55

All the oceans of the world are connected. Through-out the centuries, their names have changed, but the water has just kept flowing from one ocean to another. If, say, a dolphin had a mind to, it could swim from the water off the coast of Texas, just south of Galveston, north of Corpus Christi, and then catch an eastward current around the tip of the Florida Keys, careful not to bump into Cuba or the Yucatan, then slip north across the Atlantic—no need to stop in the Virgin Isles or Bermuda, no need to stop at all until it got to the Mediterranean Sea, just off the coast of France at the mouth of the Riviera. It could swim all that way without ever having to backtrack or take a train or hitchhike.

As a seagull flies, it's about five thousand miles, give

or take a few. It's probably a little farther for a dolphin.

Once there, that same dolphin would find an ancient swimmer, so old there are wrinkles on top of his wrinkles.

Under the moon's bright light, the dolphin darted by, and the swimmer felt his aged heart rush.

Had he just felt what he thought he felt? He paused and let the water hold him up. Yes, there it was again! A signal. At first it seemed oh-so-faint, but as he cocked his head to the wind, he felt it grow stronger. Yes. He was sure of it. Someone had made a wish on the *porte-bonheur*. A sliver of joy buzzed through his body. How many years had he been searching for this signal? Eighty? Ninety? A hundred? He didn't think it was a hundred, but he had quit counting long ago.

He ducked into the warm sea, then popped back up and shook his head. Yes, the signal was growing. He stood up in the water and tried to figure out which direction it was coming from. He stretched his arms

above his head and reached into the clear blue sky, let the wind blow through his fingertips.

Texas.

He frowned. Texas? How many times had he swum along the coast of Texas, and always to no avail? But now, tonight, he was certain, a wish had been made.

He leaned back and floated atop the warm water. The wind danced above him. A wish. Yes. It was clear and lovely.

Texas. Again.

Perhaps, he thought, *perhaps*. A smile spread across his wrinkled face, and he laughed right out loud.

56

The swimmer was not the only one receiving a signal on that blue moon night. In the house where Dogie lived, Too raised his head from the pillow where he slept between the headboard and Dogie's noggin.

Too had a title: Storm Prognosticator. A prognosticator is someone (or some dog) who can predict things. Too predicted storms, or more accurately, he predicted atmospheric disturbances, which, if you think about it, indicate some sort of storm or another.

Whenever there was a storm on the horizon or some other disturbance in the atmosphere, Too could not stop barking: "Yep, yep, yep." Plus, he danced on his tiny hind feet. Too looked a little like a Chihuahua, but had a rounder nose, and the black spots of a Dalmatian. He had enormous eyes. Maybe it was his enormous eyes

that let him see the storms coming before everyone else.

Dogie had never had a dog like Too. He was his best dog ever, just like BD. In fact, his whole name was Best Dog Too, but Dogie just called him "Too." So that's what everyone else called him.

Too.

Storm Prognosticator.

Now he raised his head above the pillow and sniffed the air. Yep, yep, yep, a storm was brewing. He could only barely smell it. Then he sniffed again. There was something different about this storm. It wasn't a typical gale that would blow in off the gulf and toss the palm trees around. No. What kind of atmospheric disturbance was this? He sat up and let the soft air of the night slip over him.

He turned in a circle on the pillow. A storm was coming, a disturbance in the atmosphere. But for now it felt far away and faint. He pushed his nose into Dogie's fuzzy dreadlocks and went back to sleep. *Soon,* he thought as he drifted into his best dog dreams, *someone will need to wake up.*

57

Anyone who lives by the sea knows that the moon is the queen of the tides. She pulls them back and forth, to and fro, up and down. Then round and round she goes.

As he sat on the lap of his old, old friend Mr. Beauchamp, Sinbad listened to the man's shallow breathing and made a great big wish, a tarpon-size wish—no, a whale-size wish, a wish as big as the moon herself, that at last Mr. Beauchamp would get his own wish, even without the night-blooming cyrus . . . before it was too late.

In the old man's hand was one of the broken blossoms. It wouldn't open now, not after crashing onto the crushed oyster shell drive.

Mr. Beauchamp had lived along this road for such a long time. He and ten wild ponies had come across

the Atlantic Ocean and across the Gulf of Mexico on a small ship from his home village of Saintes-Maries-de-la-Mer in the Camargue region of southern France, a region famous for its sturdy ponies.

Mr. Beauchamp had never meant to stay on Oyster Ridge Road this long, never. He was supposed to stay with the ship only until the crew delivered the ponies to a circus based in Galveston. He was barely fifteen when he signed on as the ship's stable boy for the journey across the Atlantic.

Mr. Beauchamp had loved the ponies. And they loved him. They knew him for his quiet touch, for his calm and steady voice, and for the way he calmed them down when the boat tossed about on the bounding seas.

But he was never supposed to stay along this stretch of the Texas coast, and he probably wouldn't have if his ship had not run aground on the sandbar just off the shore, the same one that Cabeza de Vaca hit five hundred years earlier. Not the first, not the last. The night had been stormy, and Mr. Beauchamp's ship began to take on water. The ponies panicked, he had to rush to get them off the boat safely, and once on shore, they had disappeared into the salt grass marshes so like the Camargue, the region they had left behind in France.

But something else was left behind in France. Some-one else.

Someone whose eyes were as blue as the sky, hair as black as night.

Now, all these years later, Mr. Beauchamp held the broken flower in his hand and let himself remember.

58

Two boys.

Henri Beauchamp first saw Jack in a market beside the plaza in his village, Saintes-Maries-de-la-Mer, named for three biblical Marys who had arrived there by sea.

One night after Henri had fed and watered the ponies, just weeks before he was to sail with them across the Atlantic Ocean to a place called Texas, he washed his face, slipped on his new jacket, and walked to the plaza. When a boy is fifteen and preparing to sail away, his step is light, his heart is wide open, he is ready for life to begin.

He is too excited to sleep.

The streets were quiet this late at night. There was a tavern owner sweeping the steps of his bar after the last customer had left and the baker locking his door for the night. The church bells struck eleven. Henri Beauchamp looked toward the bell tower and then at the courtyard.

There, in a circle of light made by a small lantern, stood Jack. He stood in front of the fountain, facing out. In his hand was a pocketful of coins that he tossed over his shoulder and waited to hear them splash. *Plink, plink, plink.* They made a cheerful sound, as if they were hitting the keys of a toy piano.

Henri had never seen anyone like him, never seen a face as beautiful as his.

Henri caught his breath. He felt bedazzled.

Bedazzled.

What a wonderful word.

And all around, the night-blooming cyrus opened their enormous flowers and filled the air with scent, an aroma so thick, it made the two boys dizzy.

Night after night, the two of them met at the fountain, late, after all the merchants and other townsfolk locked up their stalls and slipped into their cottages, after everyone else was sound asleep, except perhaps

for the baker, who was too busy to notice two boys out late at night.

There by the sparkling fountain they talked for hours and hours. What did they talk about? Everything! About ponies and circuses and night-blooming flowers and the whole wide world and . . . and . . . and one night, after they ran out of talk, Jack reached in his pocket, drew out a handful of coins, and threw them into the fountain, just as he had on that first night that Henri saw him.

"What are you doing?" asked Henri.

"Making a wish," he replied.

With that, Henri reached over and took Jack's hand. Jack wrapped his own fingers between Henri's.

One wish, granted.

The next morning, just as the sun arose, just before they had to part, a cat darted out from behind the fountain and ran betwixt and between their legs, making a tangle of feet and elbows and knees.

As suddenly as it had appeared, the cat vanished behind the fountain, and a moment later a large, stout woman carrying a basket of too-ripe fish in her hand trundled up. She marched directly toward the two boys. She forced her way between them and stopped.

Henri looked right into her face. She had a million lines carved into her skin. He had never seen anyone so old. From her basket, he could smell the rancid odor wafting up from the dead fish. He wrinkled his nose. She looked hard at him. Then she turned her gaze to Jack. Jack stepped back and covered his face with his arm. "Ma'aama," he stammered.

Henri couldn't figure out what was happening, only that Jack seemed to know this old woman. Was she his mother? He pushed himself off the ground and reached for Jack.

"Stop!" said the old sea wife, brushing his arm aside. Then she held her hand out to Jack. "Do you not have somethin' for your old Ma'aama?" she asked.

Jack blushed, then he felt in his pockets for a coin or a kerchief, anything he could offer to her, but his pockets were bare.

She started laughing, but it wasn't a nice laugh. "You *got* your wish, yes?" nodding toward Henri. Then she added, "But you got nothin' *more* for your Ma'aama?" Jack's face turned pale in the thin light of the night. Then the woman turned and looked again at Henri. Her gaze made him feel as though he were shrinking. Then she crossed her arms and told him, "He'd not be your kind, mon."

"Don't listen to her," cried Jack. "She's just an old fisherwoman."

When Henri glanced over the old woman's shoulder and into Jack's face, his heart pounded against his chest. All he could see were Jack's blue eyes and his expression of fear. Did he know this old crone? he wondered again. He'd called her "Ma'aama."

"He'd not be your kind," she said again to Henri.

"Pay no heed to her," Jack insisted.

Henri was confused. The old woman stared at him. Finally, he found his words. "Be gone with you, fair mother," he said, in the same gentle voice he used with his ponies.

She shrugged. "I be going, that's for sure." Then she glanced back at Jack, his hands in his pockets. He was looking down at his feet, not at her. "Nothin' here for this old woman," she said. She rubbed her enormous round belly and started to laugh again.

"Fair enough," said Henri. The old woman stopped

laughing and licked her lips, then she grabbed her basket of fish in both hands and trundled off. He watched as she disappeared at the end of the plaza. Then he saw that the black-and-white tom, huge among cats, was back. The cat's tail twitched from side to side.

Henri brushed aside what the old woman had said: "He'd not be your kind."

"Pay no mind," he started to say, but when he looked away from the cat, Jack was gone. Vanished.

Something else he couldn't see in the pale light of morning: the cat had only one eye.

Now, all these years later, Mr. Beauchamp, his face as wrinkled as that long-ago fisherwoman's, sat on his porch and stirred in his sleep, far, far from that fountain in Saintes-Maries-de-la-Mer. He stroked Sinbad. "We've been here for an awfully long time, haven't we?" Sinbad blinked his single eye and purred.

Yes, thought the cat, *an awfully long time*.

59

Just as Keeper was beginning to think it was taking an awfully long time for the boat to reach the channel of the Cut, all at once, it was only fifty feet in front of her. She gulped. From where she sat, the opening looked majorly small. Was the Cut too narrow for *The Scamper* to slip through? A quick thread of panic slipped through her. What if she got stuck? Would the boat fill up with water and sink? What then? Would it block the tides from coming and going? How would she get unstuck if, in fact, she got stuck?

Her mind raced through a whole litany of what-ifs, and all the while, the boat slipped closer and closer to the mouth of the ditch.

"Cripes!" she said, which was another word she was

not actually allowed to say out loud. "Cripes!" she repeated.

But then she remembered . . . the manatee!

For Keeper, the world unto itself was filled with signs. The clouds were signs of weather. The jelly-fish, with their stinging tails, were signs of warning. A pink ribbon was a sign too, Keeper knew that, a sign that Signe loved her.

Still, none of those signs had anything to do with mermaids, did they? But how else could she explain the manatee? Mr. Beauchamp himself had told her that in the lore of the mer, manatees often accompany mermaids. Even Christopher Columbus, in his travels to the Caribbean, suggested that manatees and mermaids swam together. Spot one, and the other should be close behind.

"Manatees are huge," she said to BD, still curled at her feet. "Like baby elephants," she added.

How, then, she had asked Mr. Beauchamp, had the manatee, the one she had seen in the Cut only a few days ago, gotten in there, gotten through the tight ditch of the Cut?

"Some things," Mr. Beauchamp had told her, "can't be explained."

Keeper took a deep breath. Even at high tide, the water in the pond was shallow, probably no more than four or five feet at its deepest point. If she stepped out of the boat, she would likely feel the bottom, even if she had to point her toes, without going under. And the water that flowed through the ditch was even shallower.

It was far too shallow for a manatee.

But shallow or not, a manatee was what she saw. She had been standing on her porch, slurping a lemon Popsicle and watching the drips from it slide down the back of her hand and finally land on the oyster shells below. BD leaned against her, his tongue dripping like the Popsicle. Quicker than a sand flea, he reached up and gave her Popsicle a stealth kiss.

"Grrrr . . . ," Keeper said. Then she added, "You might be the only dog in all of creation who loves lemon Popsicles." BD wagged his tail in agreement. She let him have another lick. The summer air was as still as a stone.

That's when she heard the splash coming from the direction of the pond. If there had been even a tiny breeze, a wisp of a breeze, she might not have heard the splash at all. Wind has a way of erasing sounds.

But on that windless day she heard it. *Splash!* She looked up from her Popsicle just in time to see a huge creature, one she had never seen before, roll up onto the top of the water and then disappear again. She squinted in the midday sun. The glare off the water was blinding.

Sploosh! There it was again. Huge and grayish brown. Enormous. A whale but not a whale. A walrus but not a walrus. But before she could move, before she even could run down the steps to the side of the pond, before she could call out to Signe, the gigantic creature vanished. Still, she knew what she had seen.

"A manatee," she told BD.

It was a sign.

For the rest of the day she sat on the end of the pier with BD, looking out at the rising and falling water of the Cut, but the manatee did not reemerge.

Later, when she told Signe what she had seen, Signe just said, "Maybe . . . it's a possibility." Then she added, "But it's not likely, Keeper. Manatees live in Florida and the West Indies. They hardly ever wander this far west."

But Keeper knew differently.

Now, as she drifted closer to the channel, she thought of the manatee. If she'd seen a manatee, there should be a mermaid.

"They travel together," Mr. Beauchamp had said.

So there it was. Another sign. She was sure of it.

A manatee couldn't get through the narrow Cut. But it had.

6⃠

Inside his orange and yellow house, Dogie felt Too's cold, wet nose on his cheek, but he didn't open his eyes. Instead, he patted the little dog on his head and rolled over. The day had been too long, and all he wanted to do was sleep. He pulled the sheet up to his chin. Maybe he would sleep for the rest of the summer, for the rest of the year, for the rest of his life.

The turmoil of the day just done washed over him. It had started with so much promise.

There he'd been, already on the beach before the sun rose. As he stood at the water's edge, the grass from the marsh behind him rustled in the morning breeze.

Then he threw his circular net out over the waves and watched it sink, leaving a checkered pattern on the water's surface. He waited a moment, then he slowly began dragging it in to shore. Behind him, Too sat in the sand and watched. Too did not like to get wet. Just like BD, he was not a sea dog. So he sat well back near the dunes in order to keep the occasional rogue wave from catching him off guard.

Dogie tugged at the heavy net. He knew there were crabs caught in its webbing. He felt them scuttling about, trying to escape. Not today. He had promised Signe that he would catch crabs for her gumbo.

Blue moon gumbo, on a blue moon night!

"P-p-perfect!" he told Too. He had been waiting for this night, the night to sing his two-word song for Signe. And now, with the gumbo, it'd be even better. He thought he'd been waiting his entire life for this one night, such an important night. A smile spread across his face, a smile as big as the sea.

Signe. He hummed his song. Would she say yes? He hummed a little louder. *Yes,* he thought, *say yes.*

Yes, yes, yes.

As he pulled the seine closer to his feet, he could see

the crabs' pinchers snapping at the tough ropes. The blue crabs that roamed this part of the coast were feisty. Anyone who has ever spent any time swimming in the Gulf of Mexico has probably felt the snip of a blue crab on their toe or ankle.

As he dragged the net in, he counted. One. Two. Three. Four. Five. Six. Seven. Eight. Nine. Ten.

Exactly ten.

Exactly perfect.

Exactly the way he felt.

Yes.

When the seine was completely out of the water, he flipped it over, and one by one, he reached underneath each snapping crab from behind and dropped it into the large aluminum tub, filled a quarter of the way up with salt water. Too walked toward the tub to inspect.

"W-w-watch out!" Dogie warned. Snip! Too barely missed a pinch on the nose. Then, angry that the crab had tried to attack him, he ran around and around the tub in circles. "Yep, yep, yep!"

Dogie laughed. "L-l-let's go, Too." The water in the tub sloshed from side to side. Dogie took a moment to steady it.

"B-b-big day, b-b-buddy," he said.

As if to say he knew that, Too barked again, "Yep, yep, yep!"

Dogie laughed, and then in Too's own language, he agreed, "Yep!"

Too loved it when Dogie spoke his language, even though there was only one word in that language, "yep." It was an all-purpose word and generally promoted health and well-being. Too said it over and over and over, all the way to the haint blue house, where Signe was already awake, stirring the brown roux that would make the base for her famous gumbo. Famous, that is, to the residents of Oyster Ridge Road, the world unto itself.

All summer Dogie had waited for this day and this night. He had practiced his two-word song for weeks. Two words. "Marry me." That was all. A simple song.

Why Dogie had never said these two words to Signe

was hard to say. He had tried before. But every time Dogie had gotten close to asking, he had swallowed the words. They simply would not come out. And just when it seemed like they might, like he might blurt them out, his tongue got all tangled up inside his mouth. Signe would blush and turn away.

Finally, it was Keeper who looked at him one day, and out of the clear blue she said, "If you ever have something important to say, you should sing it!"

Of course! He never stuttered when he sang. All he needed to do was sing two words. "Marry me." He would sing them over and over.

But now?

Everything had come undone. There had been no gumbo and no two-word song. Only a long, hard day filled with disappointment and sorrow.

Now, in his bed, Dogie rolled onto his back. He felt Too press his wet nose against his neck. He opened his eyes and glanced out the window. The sky was clear. If there was a storm, it was still far in the distance.

Dogie closed his eyes and let the night call up its sleeping air. Let it curl up on his chest just as Too curled up on his pillow. "M-m-maybe tomorrow, T-T-Too," he whispered.

Maybe.

61

Keeper's pulse was racing. At last, at last, *at last*, it felt like *The Scamper* was gaining speed. It was gunning for the channel, just like that big surfboard called the "gun." Keeper leaned forward, as if she could urge the boat to move faster. "Come on," she coaxed.

Then she made a quick decision. She had just enough time to make another wish. She scrambled for the shoe box and found another of the miniature figures. It was the *Meerfrau*.

She loved the little *Meerfrau*. Her apron covered her ample chest and waist, hiding her fishy tail.

Before Keeper could change her mind and put the figurine back in the box, she pulled her hand back, and with all her might, she tossed it into the water. "Here you go, Big Mama!" she called.

Almost in the same split second that Keeper heard the carving plink into the water, a large bead of regret landed on her shoulders. The *Meerfrau* wasn't a creature of the sea at all, but a freshwater being, like from a lake in the middle of the old forests of Germany. Had it been mean to throw a freshwater *Meerfrau* into the salty old ocean, even if the Cut wasn't exactly the ocean, but it was still salty? Keeper hoped not. She wrapped her arms around her waist and grabbed her elbows.

At her feet, BD was hunkered under his pup-tent life vest. Captain leaned against him, his feathers in disarray.

Suddenly, the wind rose up and bumped against the boat's side, making it rock. BD whined, *Please, please, please! Let's go back!* He sat up and gave her knee a stealth kiss. The boat rocked from side to side. Keeper grabbed on to him to help steady herself, and then, like that, the wind sat down again.

Keeper scanned the surface of the water, but she didn't see anything except the waves. Was something under there?

"Don't be mad at me, Yemaya," Keeper pleaded. The last thing she needed was yet another person to be mad at her, especially someone as powerful as Yemaya.

Mr. Beauchamp had told her that if Yemaya was mad, she could conjure up a storm just like that. And he'd snapped his fingers to make the point.

Keeper tugged on her life vest. She tugged on BD's too. Could Yemaya blow them right out of the boat? What would happen then?

Keeper knew how to swim. In fact, she was a pretty darned good swimmer. Every summer Signe had taken her into town to the Tater Municipal Swimming Pool and signed her up for lessons. But swimming in the pool, with its clear, chlorinated water, was a far cry from swimming in the Cut, with its to-and-fro sting-rays, or especially in the sea, with its riptides and sink-holes, its stinging jellyfish and toothy sharks.

Even though Keeper splashed along the gulf's green edge almost every day, even though she loved to jump over the shallow waves and race them in to shore, and even though she couldn't wait to learn how to surf, she hardly ever threw herself all the way in and swam in the gulf. A girl who grows up watching the surf curl itself forward and pull itself back knows all too well the hidden dangers beneath its murky surface.

And besides, Signe was not all that keen on Keeper going into the water; plus, there was that promise that Keeper had made.

As if the waves on the other side of the dunes needed to remind Keeper of all this, they lifted their voices like lions and roared. Suddenly, she couldn't help it—a great big wad of fear took hold. She clutched the oars again and winced at the blisters on her hands. Ouch!

And then—she was sure of it—she heard her name again: *Keeper. Keeper.*

Her mother?

Who else could it be, coming from the sea? She grabbed the charm, as cold as a Popsicle, colder. But there was no comfort in the icy disk.

"Who else could it be?" she asked BD.

And then all at once, it occurred to her: Jacques de Mer! A girl who grows up on the Texas coast also knows the legend of Jacques de Mer.

62

Every landscape has its magical beings. The ancient forests of the pacific northwest have Sasquatch. The piney woods of Alabama have Bigfoot. The Texas coast has Jacques de Mer.

As the story goes, there was once a family who came to the beach to picnic for the day. The family had a mother and a father and a little girl and a tiny boy— barely toddling, he was that small.

The boy was very quiet, and the beach was noisy, filled with the sounds of the waves brushing against the shore, the cries of the birds, and the whistle of the wind. The family spent the morning wading along the edge of the water.

The little girl ran back and forth in the waves, laughing with glee. The mother and father watched her closely. They took turns holding on to the tiny boy's hand. But the tiny boy watched his big sister and wanted to play in the waves too. Except that his mother and father kept holding his hand.

But somehow, some way, they let go. And he was so quiet. And the beach was so loud. And before they knew it, he was gone.

They were all frantic. The mother cried and cried. The father called and called. The little girl curled up on the sand into a small ball, as small as she could, and hid her face.

Soon a crowd gathered and lots of people helped the search. To no avail. The tiny boy was gone. Vanished.

But several days later a deckhand on a nearby shrimp boat looked out beyond his nets and saw a man swim out of the water, only the man wasn't just a man. His upper body was a man. His lower body was a fish. Down his back, a large fin. A man of the sea. And in his arms, the body of the tiny boy.

The shrimper was furious. He called his mates to

the deck and pointed and called out, "He killed the boy!"

And everyone started shouting, "Monster! Kill the monster!"

No one else saw the merman, no one but the shrimper. But they did see the body of the tiny boy, settled gently at the edge of the waves, just as quiet in death as he was in life, so very quiet. And everyone was certain that a sea monster, half fish, half man, had taken the boy.

So all the blame fell on Jacques de Mer. Not on the riptides that will pull you out. Not on the sinkholes that will draw you down. Not on the tug of the waves themselves that beckon, beckon, beckon.

Beware of Jacques de Mer.

Beware.

63

BD could feel *The Scamper* picking up speed. He lowered his head between his paws. All he could do was lie in the bottom of the boat and worry. Where, oh where, he wondered, was Signe?

As if he were wondering the same thing, Captain piped up, "C'mon, c'mon!" What he meant was, *Where, oh where, is the watermelon?* But no one seemed to be paying attention.

But BD's worrying and Captain's piping could not distract Keeper from the channel in front of her. The opening was only thirty or so yards away now. She squinted her eyes so as to assess the situation a little better. Yes, the mouth looked wider. Yes, it looked like the boat could just squeeze through. "Yes!" she cried.

She waited for BD to bark with her, but there

was no response from him except for another thin whine.

The moon, a little higher in the sky now, cast a broad chunk of light over them. Keeper took a deep breath of relief. The ditch looked completely manageable.

She glanced at the box underneath the seat, then glanced ahead at the opening of the Cut and decided, yes, there was enough time. She took another of the carvings from the shoe box.

Lorelei.

If she made another offering now, it would seal the deal to get them through the channel.

Lorelei was carved out of a plank of pine. It wasn't unusual to find pine planks deposited on the beach.

"Likely came from an old house that the sea claimed," Mr. Beauchamp had told her. Keeper knew that there were lots of abandoned houses along the coast, old fishing shacks that no one used anymore. Eventually, the sea rolled up under them, picked them up, and carried them away.

First a tree, then a house, and finally, Lorelei. The plank had had three different lives. Keeper thought her Lorelei was beautiful. She was warm in Keeper's palm. Keeper pressed the carving against her cheek.

Isn't that what people do when they love someone, press a palm against their cheek? Signe did that to Keeper all the time, pressed her palm against her cheek.

Before Keeper could change her mind, she set the Lorelei in the dark water beside her boat. "Swim," she whispered.

Keeper could only barely see the tiny figure bounce on the moonlit waves. Now there were only two figurines remaining, one in the box and one in her pocket. She swallowed hard. Two. That was a very small number. Gone were Sedna, the *ningyo*, the siren, and the *Meerfrau*.

She called again to Lorelei, "Swim to Yemaya!"

Queen of the sea.

64

All at once . . .

Whoosh! As though the channel were swallowing it whole, *The Scamper* swung right into the middle of its mouth.

Finally, finally, finally! thought Keeper.

Swwooosh!

Smack! The boat bumped into the edge of the mouth. Keeper fell backward against the stern. She leaned to her left to help right the prow so that it pointed toward the middle of the channel.

Then she heard the boat creak as it scraped one side of the ditch, then the other. She pulled herself back up, then jerked her hands away from the edges of the boat to keep them from being smashed against the hard banks that rose on either side of her. An eon of daily rushing back and forth had polished the banks smooth. The exposed layers of limestone and sand sparkled in the moon's light.

At her feet, BD pressed against her. He was shaking. Or was she the one who was shaking? Keeper clamped her teeth hard, to keep them from rattling.

The Scamper was the Best. Boat. *Ever.* Dogie had reworked every single part of it, every last plank. Keeper was certain it would carry them safely to the waiting sandbar only a hundred yards from shore, which should become visible as the tide rolled back, carrying them with it.

Step I was finally under way!

A blaze of excitement surged through Keeper, and without thinking, she shouted, "I'm coming!" The shouting made her feel braver. BD's tail thump felt reassuring. A happy sound. She opened her mouth to shout again, when . . .

Bang! The prow dipped down and jammed against something under the water. Keeper tipped forward and slammed, hard, into the seat in front of her. Her hands barely caught her in time to keep her face from meeting the wooden bench.

Water trickled over the sides. Keeper pushed herself back, trying hard not to fall on top of BD.

She pulled an oar out from under the bench and pressed it against the bank. She gave a mighty shove, but she couldn't get enough leverage. Stowing the oar, she pushed against the side with her hands, scraping her already sore palms on the limestone banks. The salt water on her raw skin felt like fire.

The Scamper moved a tiny bit. Keeper pressed as hard as she could. Then, just as quickly as it got stuck, *swish*, the boat popped back up again, knocking her backward this time. A half inch of water sloshed from the tip of the boat to the back.

She would have to figure out a way to bail. But just as the thought crossed her mind, they were out, clear of the channel. Hooray!

The boat shot into the surf and bobbed there. Keeper looked behind her, but she could not see the

Cut, only the rushing water streaming out of the ditch behind her, pushing her toward De Vaca's Rock.

"We made it!" she shouted. "Whaahoo!!!"

Victory!

65

Just ahead of *The Scamper*, the falling tide streamed out of the Cut and into the gulf, rushing toward the sandbar. There the stingrays hovered on the strong currents. How many were there? Hundreds? Thousands?

Even more were on their way, flying beneath the waves, into the Gulf of Mexico. They traveled from Bermuda and St. Thomas and even the western coast of Africa. And there, riding the waves with them, the old swimmer coursed through the water. Someone had finally made a wish on the *porte-bonheur*, he was sure of it. The long fin on his back sliced through the surface of the water.

66

From his place on Dogie's bed, Too sat up and looked out the window. He could see the moon rising higher in the distance.

The breeze felt cool on his nose. He sniffed the air. *Yep, yep, yep,* he thought. There was an atmospheric disturbance afoot. He was sure of it.

He looked at Dogie, still sound asleep. Should he wake him up? He listened as the man's breath rose and fell in the calm night air. He sniffed again. Maybe it wasn't urgent yet. He would wait a little longer.

Too didn't know that just yards away, atop the quickly retreating waters of the Cut, in the small boat called *The Scamper,* his friend BD glanced up at the same moon, and made a doggy wish: *Wake up!*

Someone needs to wake up.

67

In the deep disappointment of the night, the sound of Sinbad's purr slipped into Mr. Beauchamp's ear. The cat was nestled right on his shoulder, just behind his neck. Mr. Beauchamp reached up and patted him, rubbed his silky fur. Was there anything sweeter than the sound of a purring cat?

"Ah, Sinbad," he said. Then he tried to catch his breath. The air felt thick and heavy, and he had to draw deep, deep drafts of it to get enough. It felt like his lungs were being squeezed. He coughed, and each cough brought a shot of pain.

He placed his hand over his chest. The cat purred a little harder.

On the small table beside Mr. Beauchamp sat a single piece of driftwood and, next to it, his carving knife.

He had made a few attempts to start the new figurine for Keeper, but he hadn't gotten very far. The one she had asked him to carve . . . he wasn't sure he could. So the wood Keeper had brought to him, a slender chunk of juniper, had lain there, quiet and undisturbed.

Juniper. He remembered the juniper forests of the Camargue. Maybe this very piece had come from there? It was possible.

He patted the cat again. Lately, he had felt more anxious than ever, as if he needed to make course corrections that were resisting his efforts. He gulped in a wad of air and released it as slowly as he could. Tonight, he thought, this was supposed to have been a special night. The moon was full and just as blue as could be. A night of possibility.

Instead, the night-blooming cyrus that he grew in pots on his porch were swept into a heap on the drive below. They wouldn't bloom now, not after crashing to the ground. Their absence was just as heavy as their perfume that should have filled the air. Now he felt bereft in the presence of the empty spaces where his beloved plants used to sit.

"This was our last chance, *mon ami borgne*," he said to the black-and-white cat.

He sighed. A memory of his French village slipped into his thoughts, a sweet memory of two boys holding hands in the moon's milky light.

Holding hands made him think of his young neighbors.

"He should ask her to marry him," Mr. Beauchamp said to the cat, suddenly irritated. "Should've asked her long ago."

Sinbad knew that Mr. Beauchamp was talking about Dogie. If the cat could have spoken, he would have sounded just like an echo. But he couldn't. Instead, he jumped off the chair, spread out his front toes, and stretched.

Love, thought Mr. Beauchamp. *It's not something to put off. It's too hard to find.* The old man knew this to be a true thing: Don't put off love, no matter what.

"He should ask her," he repeated. Sinbad scratched the back of his ear with his back paw and settled into a moonbeam and purred as hard as he could.

68

Nestled as he was on top of the dog, Captain was the only critter in the boat who was completely happy. The sea was his natural home, and he was glad to have his very best friend, BD, out here on the dark waves.

He raised his head to squawk, "C'mon, c'mon," but when he did, a glimmer of light caught his eye.

There. Right there. Pressed against Keeper's breastbone. He hopped off of BD's head and onto the side of *The Scamper* to get a better look. The glimmer bounced up at him again.

Why yes! He had seen that shiny object before! It was his fallen star!

He was sure it was the same one he had discovered all those years ago. *His* fallen star.

He remembered the day—oh, how many days back?

Thousands? Way before the storm and the whole window incident. Way before he broke his wing. Back when he was in his most radiant prime.

There he was, skimming over the shallow water, looking for a tasty bite—a clam or a small crab or an itty-bitty sea turtle—when there it was, gleaming just below the water's surface.

He saw the sparkle of it smiling up at him. It was beautiful, all round beneath the water, a perfect fallen star. That's what it had to be! After all, he had seen stars falling into the ocean all his life, and he had always, *always* wanted one. But they were too fast and far away for him to catch.

All at once, every feather in his entire body, every bone, every muscle, every tingling talon wanted it. All seagulls love shiny objects, and he was no different. He was, in fact, a classic seagull.

He flew over the star, back and forth, back and forth, admiring it, until finally, he swooped down and picked it up. It was heavy in his beak, but that didn't matter. When he picked it up, a chill zipped through him from stem to stern. Nevertheless, he hung on to it.

Possession of a fallen star would raise his stature in the gull community. As far as he knew, none of the other gulls on this strip of beach had an object as lovely as this one. While he spiraled into the sky, the shiny fallen star gleaming in his beak, thoughts of acclamation in his head, he became more and more pleased with his wonderful new acquisition.

But then he was duped by a single chunk of watermelon. That's right. Watermelon was his downfall.

As he flew down the beach, he noticed a tall woman stretched out on a beach towel, sunbathing. Next to her was a bowl of something juicy and red. Something fruity. He smelled its delicious aroma as it wafted up into the air. Hallelujah, brothers and sisters! *Watermelon!* His favorite food of all time. He looked down and saw that she had a huge bowl full of it. Oh frabjous day, calloo callay.

Two events of good fortune in one short afternoon. And while he flew by, the sunbathing woman reached into the bowl and tossed a huge, juicy, ripe, red, delicious, mouthwatering chunk of watermelon into the sky in front of him.

Here's something to know about seagulls: They have very short attention spans. As soon as that watermelon rose into the air in front of him, Captain completely forgot about the star in his beak. He forgot about everything except . . . watermelon!

Without even thinking, he opened his beak just in time to catch the tasty morsel as it rose into the sky, and as he grabbed the juicy melon, the wonderful fallen star, all shiny and round, fell out of his beak and right into the hand of the tall woman.

He gulped down the watermelon and circled back around. But it was too late. He saw the surprised look on her face, saw her smile, and then saw her put his star in her beach bag, out of sight. He couldn't see the gleam of it anywhere.

But, to his delight, the tall woman called out to him, "Thank you!" and she tossed another chunk of melon straight into the sky, straight up into his beak. He swallowed it and made a large aerial circle around her. And sure enough, while he circled, she lined up a dozen chunks of watermelon on the foot of her towel. A feast!

"C'mon, c'mon!" he cried, and then *swoosh*, down he went.

Soon his belly was so full, he could barely lift himself off the ground. In his watermelon frenzy he had forgotten all about the star. That was so long ago. He had also forgotten about the tall woman. He had never seen her again after that day.

But right now, on a small boat at sea, he was certain that the object around Keeper's neck was the same fallen star that he had recovered all those years ago.

He fluffed his feathers up as fully as he could and shook his head. There was the star all right. But where was the watermelon?

"C'mon, c'mon!" he shouted at Keeper.

69

BD wished he were braver. As he hunkered down in the boat, he wished he had enough gumption to take the rope, jump overboard, and pull them all back to the pier. That was BD's wish.

But, as pointed out before, BD was not a water dog. Not one of those spaniel types who lives for jumping into the drink. Not BD. For now, all he could do was hunker down in the bottom of the boat.

Why didn't somebody wake up?

70

That morning as Signe had stood at the kitchen sink, the steam from the ruined gumbo settled on her skin. How could she have known, when she climbed into the green Dodge station wagon with Meggie Marie almost eleven years ago, that she would still be here? The Dodge was still here too.

On that day so long ago, she had waited until her grandparents were gone, maybe to the grocery store, maybe to town to visit friends, she couldn't remember, she only knew that she had to go. But when she got to the end of their driveway, she turned around. An overwhelming sense of loss curled around her and tugged her back. She needed something, anything, to take with her. So she hurried back into the house, and the first thing she saw was the bowl. Her mother's wooden bowl.

When she had been a little girl, her mother had set her in this very bowl, on the kitchen floor, and spun her around and around. It was a happy memory.

She grabbed the bowl and ran. Ran as fast as she could. Ran down the road of her neighborhood, with its tall trees and its neat yards, ran away to the highway.

Signe climbed into the car and did not look back.

Meggie Marie just let Signe be. Instead of questions, she turned up the radio and blasted down the road, letting the wind blow her long black hair behind her. With only a few words like "Wanna stop for a minute?" and "How about a Coca-Cola?" and "Let's pull over and look at the stars," the girl at the wheel and the girl with the wooden bowl became friends.

For seven years Signe and Keeper had been waiting for Meggie Marie to come back. And Keeper? Signe had let her believe that her mother was a mermaid.

Suddenly, the heat in the kitchen had seemed unbearable. Signe took a deep breath, sucked in the hot air of the room. She rubbed her fingers on each of the two halves of the wooden bowl. It was cleanly split.

And as much as the bowl reminded Signe of her own mother, it also reminded her of Meggie Marie and that night she left. Signe felt her face redden. She was *still* angry with Meggie Marie, angry with her for putting Keeper in so much danger, angry with her for leaving, angry with her for missing out on the wonder that was Keeper.

She set the pieces of the bowl next to the sink. Then, with her hands on the tiled rim of the counter, she bent over and rested her forehead on her arm.

She had not asked for this house, and she had not asked for Keeper, either, but they had been left to her by someone who had saved her life.

Signe knew that if she had stayed in Iowa, she might have died like her mother, without ever seeing the world beyond the cornfields and grain silos of the Midwest. Signe's mother had always told her, "I want to see the ocean before I die," and she never got the chance.

Yes, Meggie Marie had saved Signe, and then she entrusted her with the house and the girl. And Signe had kept them.

That had been the charge. The last thing Meggie Marie had said to her. The very last thing.

71

While the moon rose in the sky, more stingrays gathered behind the sandbar. There they came, a long stream of them moving in from Jamaica and another stream from the Virgin Islands. They were congregating, their wide wings stretched out to catch the ocean currents.

Later tonight, they would ride the tide through the narrow ditch that ran between the gulf and the pond. Who knew why they chose this sandbar or this pond or this night? Maybe it was some ancient calling? Maybe it was just an accident of the ocean's currents?

It's hard to say, but as the night wore on, more and more and more would gather through the hours. A conflagration, a congregation, a jubilation of stingrays! Come to lay their eggs in the light of July's blue moon.

Mermaids' purses.

72

Keeper blinked. It was bright out here in the surf compared to the pond. The phosphorescence of the waves gave off a glow that lit up the whole beach. Everything felt huge—the sky, the air, even the moon seemed twice as big as it had seemed when they were on the pond.

"We did it!" she said again.

Her perfect plan was working! *Step H*, check! She sat up straight, her shoulders back, her arms in the air. She felt wildly triumphant. "We're almost there!" she cried to BD, and gave him a happy hug.

He licked her right on the mouth.

"Stealth kisser." She laughed.

In the dimness the waves looked soft. The moon's beams glittered on them as they curled. And there, a hundred yards in front of her, its bony ridge gleaming in the light of the full, round moon, she saw De Vaca's Rock.

With the sandbar in her sights, Keeper grabbed the oars. She had to make sure that the boat's nose was pointed directly into the oncoming curls. If not, they'd likely turn her sidewise, and over she'd go, dog and all. She slipped the oars into the oarlocks, wincing at her raw palms.

Sploosh! The nose of the boat reared up in front of her. And just like that, one of the oars popped out of its lock and flew away.

"Oh no! Come back!" Keeper cried, her hand waiting there in midair, as if it expected the oar to fly back into it. She watched in disbelief as it tumbled into the surf.

She would have to work twice as hard now to keep the boat aimed at the sandbar. Could she get there with only one oar? She was pretty sure she could . . . that was how kayakers paddled, didn't they? One oar? And what about canoers? Again, one oar?

De Vaca's Rock jutted up in the water. Not that far.

She could make it if she just kept the boat pointed toward it. And the water here was still shallow, maybe three feet at most. Why, she could practically wade there!

But here's the thing: A riptide does not have to be deep to be strong. Keeper did not take that into consideration. A riptide that ran like a freight train just in front of that famous sandbar, a riptide that grabbed *The Scamper* with its girl and its dog and carried them

past the sand bar,

past the congregating stingrays,

past the line of breakers,

and into open water.

That riptide.

Before Keeper knew what was happening, *The Scamper* was well past the sandbar, leaving the gentle beach breakers in its wake and darting out to sea. Deep sea.

And the dog? All he could do was howl in the silvery spray of the water and wish that someone, *anyone*, on Oyster Ridge Road would wake up.

Now!

73

Unaware that she was alone, Signe dreamed in the haint blue house. A familiar dream, a memory dream. There she was, tugging at Meggie Marie's arm, begging her to get out of the water, to come back to shore, tugging at her as hard as she could. But too late. Meggie Marie began to scream, "It's coming, it's coming, the baby is coming!"

And then, like that, the baby came, slipped out of Meggie Marie and bobbed up onto the surface of the sea, right into Signe's arms, and in the very next second there was Dogie, like Neptune himself, his wet dreadlocks shining in the morning sun, throwing off the water.

She thought she probably fell in love with him that very moment, just like she knew she fell in love with Meggie Marie's baby.

But she didn't realize that she had fallen in love with Dogie then—no, she didn't. She didn't realize it for a long, long time. Instead, what she realized was that she was holding a brand-new baby in her arms, right there in the Gulf of Mexico, off the Texas coast near a tiny town called Tater, somewhere between Galveston and Corpus Christi, the waves bumping against them. There are babies who are born *at* sea, of course. Everyone's heard about them, born on boats. But how many are born *in* the sea itself?

Signe stood there in those same salty waters and looked down at the baby in her arms. A girl. She was holding a baby girl. "Hello, Sweet Pea," Signe whispered into the baby's ears. Signe's voice was the first voice that Keeper ever heard. And ever since, it was the first voice she heard in the morning and the last voice she heard at night.

Signe had watched as Dogie had cut Keeper's umbilical cord with his pocket knife, then lifted Meggie Marie in his arms and carried her back to the beach, past the Bus, and then all the way to their house on Oyster Ridge Road.

He left his surfboards and beach umbrellas unattended. Left the beach and the waves. And Signe followed him, the baby girl in her arms, all the way to that house. She probably fell in love with Dogie that day. But first she fell in love with the baby girl.

What she didn't dream about was how that baby girl, now ten and tall, was heading back to sea.

Oh, Signe, wake up!

74

"Come back!!!" Keeper cried. From over her shoulder, the sandbar grew smaller and smaller. In less time than it took for a frog to zap a fly, she had scooted right past it. The tide that had been so slow pulling her across the Cut now yanked her out into the deep water too fast.

"Stttooopppp!!!" she shouted. She was way beyond the row of breakers that lined the beach, exactly *not* where she was supposed to go.

Exactly.

She grabbed the single oar with both hands now, ignoring the pain. Dip, pull, dip, pull, dip, pull. She tried to turn the boat around, but just as the nose began to come around, the waves knocked her back.

She tried harder. Dip, pull, dip, pull, dip. Her arms

were throbbing, she was pulling so hard. But still the boat rushed away from the sandbar and the shore behind it. Within moments, they were so far out, Keeper could only barely see the silhouettes of the rooftops on Oyster Ridge Road.

Not, not, not part of the plan, she thought.

She pulled the oar into the boat. Drops of water pearled in the moon's light and dripped back into their home, the deep, enormous Gulf of Mexico.

She stowed the oar, then crossed her arms, tucking her sore hands up under her armpits. She bit her bottom lip and tried hard not to cry.

Then, in her smallest voice, she spoke her mother's name: "Meggie Marie."

She did not hear her name in return.

BD stood up and turned in a circle, then another, making the boat rock even more. Finally, he sat back down, the too-big life vest up around his ears.

That's when Keeper noticed that Captain was missing.

75

Back on shore Mr. Beauchamp barely moved in his chair on the porch. The late-night air seemed to lean against his chest.

He wished again, just as he did every night, that he could go back in time, go back to that night long ago, the night of two boys holding hands, two boys, himself and Jack, barely fifteen, their whole lives in front of them. It was a simple holding of hands, theirs was. But in that holding of hands, all that needed saying was said.

Now, as he sat on his porch, working to catch his breath, he rubbed his hands together. They felt emptier than ever.

For several days after their encounter with the old fishwife, Henri had returned to the fountain, hoping that Jack would return. He didn't understand why Jack had run away like that. Night after night, Henri returned to the fountain, and night after night, there was no sign of Jack.

The fountain. How many hand-holders had stood in the moonlight and leaned against its marble sides? Made wishes? Spoken in quiet voices?

Then at last the night that Henri dreaded arrived, the eve of his departure. On the morrow he would sail away to Texas with his Camargue ponies. He had no way of knowing how long he'd be gone. A year? Two years? His boat was bound for Galveston, but after that, it might go anywhere. He was only a stable boy, not privy to the captain's plans. When would he return? He only knew that his ship would sail at dawn. And he had no idea how to find Jack.

When Henri arrived at the fountain that last night, his heart was heavy. He waited and waited. But then, just as he was about to turn away, he felt someone's hand on his shoulder. He knew that touch.

In that moment Henri felt his whole being lift above the ground, felt the cobblestones beneath his feet fall away. In the presence of love, gravity lost its claim on Henri Beauchamp.

But their happiness was soon dashed by Henri's imminent departure. When the morning came, he would have to leave Jack behind.

Neither of them knew what to say or even how to say it. No matter how much Henri begged the sun to slow her course, the hours flew by, the night grew lighter. Finally, Henri knew he had to leave. He hung his head.

But then, while the moon stood guard, Jack reached for Henri's hand one last time and he slipped a token into it. A *porte-bonheur*. Henri felt the disk in his palm. It was the size of a large coin and hung from a thin gold chain. The gold of it gleamed in the center of his palm. Henri held it up by its chain and pressed it against his chest.

"If you ever need me," Jack said, "all you have to do is hold this in your palm and make a wish." Henri looked at the glowing disk. He curled his fingers over it. It was as warm as a sunbeam.

Henri felt a catch in his throat. He needed to say something, but he was afraid that words might ruin everything.

Instead, he slipped the token into his pocket. He could feel its warmth through the fabric of his jacket, against the skin around his waist. He swallowed hard. Then, at last, he opened his mouth and said, "Yes, I will take it with me and make a wish that you'll swim all the way to Texas and find me there." And then the two of them burst into laughter.

Fifteen. They were only two fifteen-year-old boys. When boys are fifteen, anything is possible, isn't it? Even swimming from France to Texas.

As if to seal the deal, the enormous one-eyed cat wandered up and wove himself between their legs. He purred. But when Henri bent down to rub the big tom, he heard the heavy steps of someone approaching. He glanced at Jack. Jack's face went pale in the moon's light.

"Ma'aama!" cried Jack.

There was the old sea wife from before. The strong aroma of fish rose from the basket on her arm. It stung Henri's nostrils and burnt his eyes. This time she ignored Jack and walked right up to Henri. "Here you be talkin' about wishes, but you have no gift for me?" she asked, staring right at him.

Henri spoke softly. "Begone, dear mother," he told her. But she grabbed his sleeve and glared at him with eyes the color of the ocean.

"Can't you see?" she said. "He belong to me, not you."

"But—," Henri sputtered.

She cut him off and said, just as she had the first night, "He'd not be your kind, mon."

Henri pulled his sleeve away from her wrinkled hand; the smell of dead fish pooled around his feet. He felt like he was sinking. He reached into his pocket. The *porte-bonheur* was still warm from Jack's hand.

He wasn't afraid of a wrinkled old fisherwoman, but he was confused. Who was she? He wondered again if she was Jack's mother. But in the next moment she walked directly toward Jack. Jack stepped aside to avoid her. Too late. She shoved him as hard as she could.

Jack stumbled backward, his arms spinning in circles, trying to catch his balance. Henri lunged for him, but to no avail. Jack fell straight back into the sparkling fountain. *Splash!*

"Noooo!" Jack yelled.

As he lunged, Henri lost his own balance and slipped, bumping his head against the hard curved edge of the fountain. For a moment he could see only blackness, could breathe in only the smell of dead fish. His head ached from the blow. The fisherwoman put her face right in his, then she reached down and pulled him up by his right arm and forced him to face the water.

Henri rubbed the back of his head. A flame of pain flared up just behind his eyes. He blinked. For a second he couldn't focus, everything was blurry. He shook his head, then blinked again, trying to make everything clearer. Then he remembered. Jack! Where was he? He pushed the old woman aside.

There in the fountain was Jack, facedown in the water, floating, right there on the surface.

In a panic Henri grabbed for Jack's hand, but as soon as he touched it, he recoiled in horror. The hand that he had known so well was now covered in scales. Where Jack's legs had been, a long fishy tail appeared. Down his back, a fin ran from his neck to his waist.

"You see," rasped the old woman, "he'd not be your kind, mon."

Henri shook his head again. Maybe he wasn't seeing things right? How could it be? He felt the knot on the back of his head. Maybe the blow had distorted his vision? Henri refused to believe his eyes, and yet— he watched Jack transform. Was this really Jack? It couldn't be. But when he looked again, he saw . . .

"Monster!" he rasped.

He took a deep breath. He choked on his own words. "Monster!" he croaked again.

He'd heard all the sailors' tales of the people of the sea, those creatures who wore the skins of humans, sirens who lured their victims to their deaths, dashed against the rocks and jetties of the jagged shorelines, enchanters, real but not real.

He'd never believed the tales to be true, just amusements to pass away the long, lonely stretches at sea. And yet, here was Jack, changing before his eyes.

Monster!

He couldn't bear it. All this time, he had thought that the affection between him and Jack was real. But when he looked again at the floating creature in the fountain, he couldn't see Jack at all; instead, all he saw was the long fin down the creature's back, the shiny scales that ran from his shoulders down his arms and around his chest. Betrayal blazed through his body, it wrenched his stomach inside out. He backed farther away.

The old woman stood by the fountain and laughed. "You see, he'd not be your kind, mon!"

"Henri!"

He heard Jack call his name.

"Wait!"

Henri paused. He heard it again, his name.

"Henri!"

The voice was so familiar. Jack's voice.

Henri turned away. His face burnt, shame curled around his neck and throat. How could he have been so naive? He'd actually thought that what he and Jack shared was real. He began to run, his legs trembling, all the way to the docks, where he ran up the ramp of the steamer, its hold filled with wild ponies, ponies from the Camargue.

He did not look back. Not then. He only looked down. Down at his feet, down at the straw of the ship's stable. Down.

The next morning the boat set sail. One boy, only fifteen, heartsore, walked to the edge of the rail. The water churned beneath him. His eyes burnt from the tears that he had shed all night. His throat ached. He'd stared out toward the harbor and then to the open sea, refusing to look at the place he was leaving.

But for some reason, somewhere inside of the turmoil and betrayal, something inside him spoke up. *Turn around,* it whispered to him. He rubbed his eyes and slowly glanced over his shoulder. There, on the very end of the dock, sat the one-eyed cat. Before he could stop himself, Henri waved. And he couldn't say for sure, but he thought he saw the cat wink with his one good eye.

Exactly then Henri knew he had made a mistake. He should not have run away. He should have stayed there by the fountain. He should have at least said good-bye.

He put his hand in his pocket and found the *porte-bonheur*, still warm. He looked back at the pier. The one-eyed cat waited. All at once, Henri Beauchamp spun on his heels and stretched his arms wide to the morning sky. It didn't matter, did it, what Jack was? It only mattered that he loved him.

76

With the shoreline receding, Keeper pressed her sore hand against her pocket. If Yemaya was so powerful, why, oh why, hadn't she helped her? After all, Keeper had given her not one, not two, not three, not four, but five—count them, five—of her most prized possessions: Sedna, the *ningyo*, the *Meerfrau*, the siren, and Lorelei. She had only two left, one of which was the likeness of Yemaya herself.

"Big Mama," she called, and she repeated her wish, "help me find my mother." Then she turned her head to see if she could hear a response.

Nothing.

Maybe, thought Keeper, Yemaya needed something bigger than a wish. "I know," she said, "a prayer."

She tried to think of a prayer, but most of the prayers that Signe had taught her were prayers of gratitude, like for blue skies and clean air and fresh cantaloupe and tiny geckos. They weren't necessarily prayers for help.

Signe was not necessarily one for asking for help.

And besides, Keeper knew, Signe would probably not think that prayers were practical. "Let's be practical, Keeper," Signe would say.

Keeper looked straight up at the moon, folded her hands together, and then out of the clear blue . . .

"C'mon, c'mon!"

Captain! He was back! Wherever he had gone during the wild ride through the channel, here he was again. Relief at the bird's appearance flooded over Keeper. Surely, if Captain was here, they couldn't be that far from land.

BD sat up. Captain landed with a little skip-skip onto the bench, then he pulled his wings in, fluffed his feathers, and screeched, "C'mon, c'mon!"

Then both the bird and the dog looked directly

at her, as if they were telling her, *Okay, this has been fun, but let's go home now.*

Home, Keeper thought. How was she going to get back there?

Keeper had not intended to ride *The Scamper* beyond De Vaca's rock. The plan was to use the tide to push her craft onto the sandbar and wait for Meggie Marie to meet her there. It was all supposed to be a snap. Nothing to it. Easy peasy.

Steps I, J, K, and L: Row to the sandbar. Find Meggie Marie. Tell Meggie Marie everything that happened. Ask Meggie Marie what to do.

That's the way the plan was supposed to go. Keeper pushed her thumb into her back pocket. The plan was still there. But it was not working. There was nothing on the plan that said: *Pass the sandbar and head out to sea.*

And how could she find Meggie Marie now? Could Meggie Marie find her? That was a thought: Meggie Marie could find *her*!

Keeper reached for the charm around her neck. She'd make another wish. That's what she'd do. And maybe she would send a small, invisible prayer to the moon too. But before she could think of what to say, a large wave picked up the boat and shook it. BD yelped. Keeper pulled on the straps of his life vest. "Hang on," she told him, and in that exact moment another wave rolled up beside them and pushed the boat sideways. Her stomach lurched.

Which way was she going now? In the direction she thought the shore should be, there was only water.

Water, water, and more water.

She couldn't even see the houses anymore, she realized

with a gasp. For a second she couldn't breathe at all. The shore had completely vanished, along with the sandbar.

Take a breath, take a breath, she told herself. She opened her mouth and pulled in a big gulp of air and looked as hard as she possibly could. But there was no sign of land anywhere. Only waves and more waves.

The moon was neither east nor west, north nor south. Instead, it was directly above, nudged against the highest point of the night sky's dome. Smaller than it had been before. Farther away than ever.

Well, she had to do *something*. Praying and wishing weren't getting her anywhere. So Keeper picked up the oar, then before she even dipped it into the water, she realized miserably that she had no idea which way to go. What if she started paddling and wound up even farther from shore? And besides, her hands were too sore to even hold it.

She let the oar drop and rested her forehead on her knees. She'd have to wait until dawn, when she could see land again. But how long would that be? Then she had a more unsettling question: What if, by that time, the waves pushed her so far out to sea that she couldn't see the shore? Then what?

And she knew, De Vaca's Rock or not, it was time to call her mother. *Step J.*

Slowly, carefully, she stood up and called out: "It's me. It's Keeper." She listened. But all she heard was the splashing of the black waves against her boat.

She called again. "I'm here! Your Keeper is here!"

She listened again, and this time she thought she heard her own name echo back at her: *Keeper. Keeper.*

Or was it the wind?

She sat back down, and when she did, the carving of Yemaya poked her in her thigh—a reminder.

"If you give her a gift, she might grant a wish." That's what Mr. Beauchamp had told her.

A gift. She had already given her five gifts. But she had more. Keeper reached beneath the bench for her shoe box. It was a soggy mess, but there was one figurine left in it. She lifted it out. "The *rusalka*," Keeper said uncertainly. The *rusalki* were tricksters. They were known for shedding their tails and climbing into trees so that they could scare unsuspecting passersby.

Rusalki never combed their moss green hair, and they loved to spin in circles. *The Scamper* spun in its own circle.

Spun. Spin. Spinneroo.

Spinning in the water.

Tricked. She felt tricked. The riptide had tricked her.

"Go," she told the carving, but before Keeper set her in the water, she planted a kiss on her head and pinned a huge hope to her own heart.

"Help me find my mother."

77

Too raised his head from Dogie's pillow for the ump-teenth time and sniffed the air. The storm that he knew was eminent was growing. Outside the window, the moon was slipping back and forth between the clouds. Was the moon sending him a message?

What was it? All at once, Too knew he needed to wake Dogie.

"Yep, yep, yep!" he barked. Then he grabbed Dogie's sheet with his tiny teeth and tugged.

78

In the haint blue house Signe stirred in her sleep. A moonbeam slipped through her window, then flickered out. The immediate darkness was sharp. Signe reached over to her nightstand and pressed down on the clock's snooze button. The green light illuminated the numbers: 12:00. Midnight.

Odd, she thought, to wake up exactly at midnight.

Then the moon, as if she were playing a game, popped back on. Signe blinked.

Just as quickly, it flickered out again. In the darkness Signe rubbed her eyes. Tomorrow, Signe decided, she would talk to Keeper. She would tell her that crabs didn't send messages, that there were no manatees in this part of the world, no sea serpents or water dragons or any other enchanted beings, no haints.

Most of all, she would tell Keeper that there were no mermaids.

Signe pulled the covers up and rolled over so that she couldn't see the beckoning moon outside her window.

From too far off the shore, BD looked up at the very same moon and wished again:

Wake up, Signe, wake up. Your girl is out at sea.

Your girl is out at sea.

79

At the house next door Too was more successful than the moon. He walked in a circle on the pillow and watched as Dogie sat on the edge of the bed and scratched his head.

"St-st-storm?" he asked, looking right at Too.

"Yep, yep, yep," barked Too.

Dogie pulled on his shorts and his T-shirt and then slipped his feet into his flip-flops.

"C-c-c-coffee first," said Dogie.

"Yep, yep, yep," said Too, but this time he didn't mean to agree. He wished like crazy that he could say, *Nope, nope, nope, no time for coffee*, but he knew that Dogie never did anything without a cup of coffee.

He barked again, "Yep, yep, yep!" and for punctuation he added a little growl.

"Okay," said Dogie. "I g-g-g-get it." But instead of walking out the door, he headed for the kitchen and the coffeepot.

"Grrrr . . ." Too trotted to the back door and sat down. He was ready to go. Ready. To. Go. "Yep, yep, yep!"

80

Across the road, Mr. Beauchamp saw the moon too. What a long night this had been. He rubbed Sinbad and slumped down in his chair. What a long time he had been here, in this house beside Oyster Ridge Road.

He couldn't remember when he had first swum ashore—how long ago was that? Seventy years? A hundred?

Where, he wondered, were all the ponies?

It was because of them that he had come to Texas, together on a large steamer that had struck the sand-bar just out from the beach. The wild ponies of the Camargue, bound for a circus in Galveston. He remembered that awful day, remembered the terrified ponies, their screams as the boat jarred and listed, then began to take on water.

One by one, he had gently led them to the side of the boat and coaxed them to jump into the water. And one by one, they had trusted him. When the last one, a charcoal gray mare, balked, he pulled himself onto her back and kicked her hard in the ribs so that she leaped off the side of the steamer, her front hooves pawing at the emptiness beneath her, until together, they crashed into the water.

Mr. Beauchamp would never forget that moment. He felt like he was on a winged horse, a Pegasus. Flight. It was wonderful and terrifying all at the same time. When they hit the water, he slid off of her back and both of them rode the waves to the sandy beach.

Ten ponies swam ashore that night and disappeared into the salt marshes of the Texas coast, so like the salt marshes of France, but with fewer trees.

Gone. All those ponies. And something else, too— a *porte-bonheur*. Somewhere between the listing boat and the beach, somewhere in the salty water of the coast, he had lost it, fallen from his pocket.

No effort was ever made to round up the ponies. As

soon as the captain of the boat was able to talk the owner of a tug into pulling him off of the sandbar, he sailed into the port of Galveston, stayed only long enough for repairs, and headed off for Egypt. Henri Beauchamp did not go with him.

Instead, he signed on with a passenger ship headed to France, back to Saintes-Maries-de-la-Mer. He had to find Jack.

He was ashamed that he had reacted so badly. What did it matter? All that mattered, all that ever had, was how much he longed to hold Jack's hand again.

When he got back to his village, he ran to the plaza with the fountain, but no one had ever seen a boy by Jack's description. Dark black hair, sky blue eyes. He even tried to find the old fisherwoman, but she also was a mystery to the townsfolk. For days and months he went to the fountain. Night after night. But Jack never returned, nor did the sea wife.

Just as Henri was about to give up, he spotted a large black-and-white cat with a single eye. The cat seemed to wink at him, then wove between his ankles.

Was it the same cat that had been in the market on that day when Jack had given him the token? Could it be? His heart pounded hard in his chest. He reached down and scratched the cat between his ears. Henri made a decision. He would sail around the world if he had to, until he found Jack.

The next week he and the cat embarked upon their journey, from London to Sydney to Vancouver to Hoi An to Auckland to San Francisco, all to no avail, until at last they made their way back to the coast of Texas. When he disembarked in Corpus Christi, the cat followed him to the shore. And in all those years Mr. Beauchamp had grown older and older.

And what about the cat? Was it the same cat year after year? The same one-eyed tom, black-and-white and huge? Mr. Beauchamp was never sure. From time to time, the cat would disappear for a stretch, then one day he'd show up again with a black spot in a different place on his coat, or an extra toe on his front paw, or most mysterious of all, the good eye would change, so that instead of his right eye being good, it would be his left eye that he looked through.

Regardless, Mr. Beauchamp's cat was always named Sinbad, after the one-eyed pirate of fame and fable.

Together, they hitchhiked north to the lonely stretch of beach beside a large pond with a deep channel that ran between the surf and the marsh. When the tide was low, they could see the sandbar where his ship had run aground, its narrow ridge just above the water's surface. This was where Mr. Beauchamp had lost the *porte-bonheur*. Maybe he could find it again.

For years he walked the beach, day after day, hoping that the tide would offer it up.

The Texas coast was where he had told Jack that he was going. Maybe, he thought, maybe, instead of trying to find Jack, Jack would find him. So he built his house and planted his roses and night-blooming cyrus. At night he could hear the ponies calling to one another.

Years and years, so many years passed that he lost track of how many times he had swum out into the surf, diving down, looking for the lost charm, so many times, until at last he was too old to wade into the water, afraid that the tide would carry him out to sea and he would not have the strength to swim back to shore.

And eventually, the ponies' voices died away too.

All he had left of Jack were the cat and the roses and the night-blooming cyrus. The roses bloomed year-round, but the cyrus, ahhh, the night-blooming cyrus. They only bloomed once a year, then only on a full moon night. They would fill the air with their spicy-sweet aroma, and their scent would remind Henri Beauchamp of Jack and those nights long ago.

But this year the cyrus would not bloom at all, and Mr. Beauchamp, the broken stalk in his hand, did not believe that he would still be here, on Oyster Ridge Road, for another blooming of the cyrus, a whole year away.

And in that moment, the moon as bright as could be, Sinbad, with his one brilliant eye, looked toward the bountiful sea.

"Hurry," he purred, "hurry."

And the girl in the boat looked at that very same moon and wished again for her mother. And again. And again. And again.

81

Meanwhile, Dogie looked at the clock in the kitchen. Midnight. No wonder he felt so groggy. He walked to the sink and filled up the coffeepot with water. He'd only had a few hours of sleep. He'd need a couple of cups of coffee, despite Too's obvious impatience.

While he waited for it to brew, he glanced at his broken ukulele. The koa wood was as shiny as it had been when his uncle gave it to him.

He frowned, then found a dishcloth and covered it. It reminded him of the way people cover a person's face after they've died. Sadness inched its way up his fingers.

He loved that ukulele.

When he strummed it, it was like the strings called out the perfect words of his songs, words that tumbled out of his mouth with no hesitation, clear and happy. No stuttering. Perfect. He had not set out to be a musician and didn't think of himself as such. Not really. But when he returned to New Jersey from the war, when his whole body could not stop shaking, his great-uncle Sylvester came over one day and handed it to him.

"Here," he said, "it was given to me when I came home from my own war." Dogie looked at the tiny instrument and couldn't say anything. Not even "th-th-thank you." His uncle didn't expect him to. He just said, "Anyone who's gone to war and lived to tell about it needs some music." He paused. "The uke should help."

Uncle Sylvester didn't offer up any other explanation, just handed it to Dogie and walked out the door.

He did not want to tell anyone about the war, about what he had seen there or heard or smelled or tasted. There was no telling about it. And besides, he couldn't make the words come out, even if he wanted to. He just sat there and shook, shook from head to toe. And the whole time, Uncle Sylvester's ukulele sat beside him, small, silent.

It sat there until Dogie's mother picked it up and handed it to him.

He let his right thumb strum lightly over the nylon strings. The instrument rang out. This is the difference between a ukulele and all of the other stringed instruments: It rings. Almost like bells, a ukulele has a crisp, ringing sound.

Dogie's had it with him ever since, kept it beside him as he drove the yellow bus along the highways and byways, until he parked that same bus in the sand along this strip of Texas beach, and every night since, he's sat on the porch of the haint blue house and played his songs, songs plain and clear, without stutters, for Keeper and Signe.

But that was before the incident with the crabs and the broken bowl and the shattered flowers and the cracked ukulele, leaving him with his unsung two-word song, and the moon as full as a bowl of gumbo.

82

A look of dismay crossed BD's face. The waves were getting taller. The wind was kicking up. The little boat was built for a gentle pond; it was no match for the Gulf of Mexico. Even the smaller waves felt huge.

They needed to find the way home. Soon.

83

Keeper scanned the water all around. And around and around and around. *The Scamper* couldn't seem to stay pointed in any one direction. Instead, it kept spinning, first one direction, then another, in sudden twists and turns. Then it would stop just long enough for her to catch her breath before it spun again. In the midst of the spinning, Keeper felt the wind pick up. The waves seemed to be getting taller.

She felt dizzy. So much spinning . . . and spinning . . . *spinneroo!*

Where was Meggie Marie? Keeper tried calling again. "Over here! We're here!" Her voice cracked. It was getting raspy.

Her mother was supposed to be out here. This

was the last place that Keeper had seen her. "Meggie Marie!" Keeper called again.

Then she listened. But there was no answer at all. Even the wind seemed to have forgotten her name. The moon, directly above her head, looked no larger than one of the bottle caps on a cold Dr Pepper.

And right then Keeper felt as small as a minnow, smaller. Where was her mother? she wondered. All these years, she had been sure that her mother was out here, watching her, waiting for her.

Where was she now?

84

Take a deep, dark night.
Take a small, small boat.
Take a lucky-charm girl.
Take a bent-winged seagull.
Take a rushing tide.
Take a big blue moon.
Add it all up.
What do you get?
One scared dog.
That's what.

85

Captain was getting weary of the boat, especially since there were clearly no snacks there. He decided to take another break from the sailing life to see if he could find some small repast to replenish his stomach.

From his perch on the boat's bench, Captain launched himself into the sky. With his wings, he pulled at the wet air above the water, higher and higher. When he looked down at BD and Keeper, they looked too small in the middle of all that water. It's not often that seagulls wish for anything that can't be eaten. But in that moment, Captain flew beyond his seagull self and wished the girl and the dog could fly, fly right on up here with him and wing their way home.

86

Below, Keeper wasn't watching Captain just then. She was watching the waves. They were most definitely getting larger.

Now would be a good time for Meggie Marie to appear. A perfect time.

"Where are you?" she called. "Where are you?" She rubbed her hands worriedly on the sides of the boat. The wood was so smooth.

And once again she had that thought that she had done this before—held the sides of a boat, a boat caught in the waves. Just like this.

But it wasn't this boat, was it?

The realization hit her hard.

It wasn't this boat.

It was another one.

A smaller one.

A long time ago.

She held on as the boat rocked between the growing waves.

She was sure she'd done this before. But when?

She scrunched down into the belly of the boat, as close to BD as she could get. BD was shivering. The moon's light was fading as it followed its arc across the night sky, and the boat suddenly gained speed. It felt like something was pushing her. Keeper sat back up and looked over the side.

She rubbed her eyes. Maybe it was just a trick in the moon's light. Maybe it was her imagination. Maybe . . . but then she saw it again on the other side of the boat.

A huge fin.

It was moving around the boat in a circle. Keeper pressed herself flat into the bottom of the boat and hugged BD to her. With her other hand, she grabbed the charm around her neck. The cold of it bit her fingertips, but she did not let go.

87

As Signe slept, the cooling night wind slipped through her window and nestled next to her on the pillows. She pulled her sheet up under her chin. She could not feel a faint tap-tap-tap on her shoulder, if there even was one.

After all, who can feel a haint?

88

From his location in the sky above the boat, Captain called, "C'mon, c'mon." It was such a bother that his humans, and particularly his dog, couldn't fly. He had tried to show them how on numerous occasions, but even though Keeper flapped her arms from time to time, it was obvious that their distinct shortage of feathers was a huge impediment.

He was glad to be soaring above the rough waters, but from his vantage point, he couldn't see the land in any direction. He felt a small twinge of worry. He had not realized how far from shore they had drifted.

Most seagulls have an innate knack for finding the beach, but Captain's bent wing tended to throw him somewhat off course. He would have to climb a little higher to see if he could spot any lights from shore.

"C'mon, c'mon," he called. And up he went, his white feathers dotted with starlight.

89

Keeper hugged BD tighter. She was gladder than ever that he was with her. She hoped whatever was circling them wasn't a shark. Could it be a shark? It couldn't be, could it? She forced herself to peek over the boat's side again. She could most definitely see a fin. It was *big*. It seemed to come closer, then disappear.

BD whined. She buried her face in his broad neck, and as she did, the boat began to rise.

Up up up *The Scamper* raced, and then just as quickly, it charged down down down again. She held on to BD as tight as she could. And all the time, the boat rose and fell, rose and fell, rose and fell as . . .

. . . Keeper clung to BD.

But Keeper's two arms wrapped around him weren't enough to keep the boat from racing up the sides of the gigantic waves and then cascading down them. They weren't enough against the pull of the churning sea, not enough to withstand the swirling water, which yanked him out of her embrace and carried him toward the stern of the boat.

BD gave a yelp. Frantic, Keeper reached for him, but not in time. The sea tugged BD away, away from Keeper, away from *The Scamper*, and hurtled him into the frenzied water, and Keeper, horrified, could only scream: "Noooo!!!! BD!!!!!!"

90

Keeper grabbed for BD. She reached and reached and reached. She leaned as far over the edge of the boat as she could, the sides of it digging into her stomach, but she could not keep her BD from flying over the side and into the water just as a huge wave lifted the boat up up up and brought it crashing back down. When she looked in every direction, the water stood above her as if she were in a deep pit. Then, just as suddenly, it lifted her again.

Up.

Down.

Up.

Down.

Up.

Down.

She slid from one side of the boat to the other, smashing first into the seat, hitting her right elbow hard, then tumbling against the stern. *Smack!* At last she grabbed the sides of the boat as hard as she could, held on with all her might, and looked over the edge. There was no sign of the orange life vest.

No sign of BD.

"BD!!!!!!!" she wailed. "BD!!!!!"

And all at once, it seemed like the entire Gulf of Mexico was nothing but her screaming voice sliding up and down the curved walls of cold, salty water.

91

BD. BD. BD. BD. Her heart thumped.
   Keeper called and called and called. No BD.
      Only a fin.
         Circling.

92

Too was becoming more and more worried. He scratched at the door. Dogie picked up his coffee cup and took a long drink.

Then, just as Too began to tremble, a gust of wind rattled the door.

"Yep, yep, yep!" He spun in a circle at Dogie's feet. Surely Dogie had heard that, surely.

As if Dogie could read Too's thoughts, he replied, "Yep, T-T-T-Too, I heard it." Too ran back and forth from Dogie to the door. *Gotta go. Gotta go. Gotta go.* On his last dash to Dogie, he licked the man's toes. Dogie laughed, then bent over to scoop Too up in his arms.

No laughing, Too thought. This wasn't funny. Something was seriously wrong in the world unto itself.

He squirmed in Dogie's arms until Dogie finally

set him down and opened the door. Then, without waiting another minute, Too ran as fast as he could to the beach.

Dogie called out, "Too! Come back!" But the little dog did not turn around.

Instead, he ran and ran and ran, leaving Dogie well behind.

93

Keeper was drenched. Her hair hung in strands down her face and stung her eyes. She pushed it back. She'd looked for BD as long as she dared, hoping against hope to spot him. But the waves grew wilder, and she was terrified that she'd fall out too. Now she lay curled up as tightly as she could in the bottom of the shuddering boat, water sloshing over her legs. She wrapped her arms around herself, the same arms that had let go of her dog.

Lost. She had lost her BD.

The Scamper bucked in the growing waves, and each time it did, Keeper felt her entire body lift up, away from the boat's bottom.

What if it threw her out too? She peered over the side once more. A scream caught in her chest. There it was again, the large fin, just there, beside her.

And then it was gone!

She blinked. Where was it? Then the worst thought ever crashed into her, worse than the worst wave: What if it had gone after BD?

Keeper moaned and wedged her body against the rear bench, tucked herself as far beneath it as she could.

94

Dogie could see that Too was frantic. As soon as he'd opened the door, the little dog shot out of his arms. Dogie stopped for a small second to let his eyes adjust to the dark. Too was far ahead of him. Dogie could only barely hear the dog's voice in the distance, and the waves from the shore were quickly drowning him out. What had gotten into him?

Dogie picked up his step. The night was still clear, only a few clouds in the starry sky. Was there a storm coming? Too had never missed one, not yet. But aside from the breeze feeling cooler than usual, it didn't seem like a storm was at bay.

Still, Too was never wrong.

Dogie would go ahead and double-check everything, but first he called out for the dog.

"Too!" He paused. He could not hear the familiar, "Yep, yep, yep!" Where was he? Dogie called again, "Too!! Heeerrrree, b-b-b-buddy!"

He listened. All he could hear was the breaking of the waves against the sand. He could see that the tide was still out. In the moon's light the sand looked as smooth as silk, brushed clean by the retreating water. The moon was in the western quadrant. She'd be setting in a few hours.

He felt a pang of regret. Blue moon. Who knew how long it would be before the moon was blue again? Months? A year? He gazed at it. And there it was again, the longing, such a longing to sing his two-word song to Signe.

He turned away from the moon. Where was Too? And then, as if in answer to his question, Too came running up. "Yep, yep, yep!" he barked.

Dogie reached for him, but Too eluded his grasp. Off he went, in the other direction.

What had gotten into that dog? Then Dogie thought he could feel the wind begin to shift. And with that, he hurried to the dark Bus. He unlocked the door and stepped up into it. The rainbow colors of the surfboards seemed subdued in the dim beam of his flashlight. He went down the aisle and checked the windows. Everything seemed shipshape.

He stepped back out of the Bus, and when he did, he noticed the silhouette of a solitary seagull skimming the water's surface. Captain? What was Captain doing out this late? He looked again. If it was Captain, he would be able to tell by his wing. But when he looked harder, all he could see was the water.

"Yep, yep, yep!" He heard Too again.

The little dog raced right up to him and began to run around his legs in circles. Dogie reached for him, but Too shot away again, only this time he ran toward the Cut.

95

Keeper stayed curled up tight as another huge wave spun her onto its back, up up up. She burrowed harder into *The Scamper's* bottom. She braced herself for the ride down the wave, and sure enough, *swoosh*, down she went.

Deeper and deeper and deeper the boat fell. Keeper's whole body tensed as she waited for the bottom of the wave's trough. How far could she fall, how deep was it?

Then, *bam!* the boat crashed into the wave's well. Keeper felt the impact in every muscle, every bone, every sinew. Her legs cramped. Her arms cramped. Her stomach cramped.

Her fingers, her sore fingers, cramped as she clung to the bench of the little boat, clung as hard as she could. She felt the charm bang against her breastbone. The last thing that Meggie Marie had given her. Just before she swam away. Just before Signe grabbed her. Signe . . . grabbed her!

Then Keeper remembered, remembered exactly. She *had* done this before . . . ridden the waves in another small boat, a boat even smaller than *The Scamper*, a round boat, a boat with smooth edges, just like this one. She had been tossed about then, too. She remembered.

Remembered. Remembered. Remembered.

The small boat. The crashing waves. The cold water.

Alone.

But not alone.

No. She had not been alone that night. She had been with Meggie Marie.

96

A large wooden bowl.

Large enough for a little girl to sit in . . .

        while her mother spun her around on the
        kitchen floor.

A beautiful wooden bowl.

Large enough for another little girl to ride in . . .

        while her mother set her afloat on the
        waves of the sea.

        Suddenly, the terrible memory washed
        over her, a blue memory, so blue that it
        ached. Her birthday night.

She was only three.

As Keeper crouched down in *The Scamper*, the memory wound itself around her like a rope.

• • •

She was in a wooden boat. But it was round and deep, with no bow or stern. It had no port or starboard, and no sail, either. And she was far from the shore, right beside the sandbar, De Vaca's Rock. Her little boat bumped against it. Tapped against the old rock.

From where she was in the water, she could barely see the flickering campfire on the beach a hundred yards away. Signe was back there, sleeping beside the fire. "Three's a charm," that's what Signe said. Instead of a cake, Signe had made Keeper's favorite, sweet potato pie, which she served with Reddi-wip, which turned out to be Sinbad's favorite too.

Everyone from Oyster Ridge Road had walked from their houses to the beach to roast wieners and marshmallows. Dogie played his ukulele, and Signe curled up on a beach towel and fell asleep to his funny song about "the little girl from the sea, who just turned three, little Sweet Pea." BD curled up next to the fire, too. He was tired from chasing Sinbad all afternoon, up and down the beach. Sinbad was tired from eating so much Reddi-wip.

Keeper wanted them to wake up and see her out there, on top of the waves. Her boat was bobbing, bobbing up and down. It was cold. All she had on was her bathing suit bottom and a new cotton T-shirt from Dogie. The bottom of the shirt was soaking up the water from the bottom of the boat.

She started to cry, but then a beautiful face popped out of the water just beside her. Meggie Marie, her mother. A tiny vein of relief entered her. Meggie Marie shook her long hair, and a spray of water flew into the air, shimmery drops above the waves' surface. At last Keeper wasn't alone. But why wasn't Signe out here with them, out here on the waves? She looked toward the campfire growing smaller. Meggie Marie smiled and looked at her. "Don't worry," she said, "we're going to ride the waves back to shore."

Then she added, "You'll see. It'll be easy peasy."

She wanted to believe her mermaid mother, but instead, she bit her lower lip. Mermaids were unreliable. Here one moment, gone the next. Meggie

Marie hummed a familiar tune: *You are my little mergirl, and I'm your mermaid mama.*

The tune. Keeper remembered.

She remembered reaching for Meggie Marie, but when she let go of the round boat, it began to rock. She grabbed the round sides again and swallowed hard. Her mermaid mama kissed the top of her head.

Then she saw the charm around her mother's neck, aglow against her soft skin. She'd never seen it before. She reached for it. "A gift from a seagull," said Meggie Marie, then she laughed and ducked under the water again. Where did she go?

All of a sudden, Meggie Marie emerged from the water, still laughing. She removed the charm from around her neck and placed it around Keeper's. "Happy birthday," she said. The cold of it startled Keeper.

The tiny boat rocked; Meggie Marie laughed. That was the thing with Meggie Marie, she was always laughing. Keeper wanted to laugh too, but she was too afraid. She was drenched and scared and wanted to go back to the beach, wanted to find her beach towel with the red and blue fish on it, the one that Signe gave her for her birthday. She wanted to find Signe and curl up on her lap.

Suddenly, Meggie Marie swam up beneath her, bumping the wooden craft with her shoulder.

"Ride the waves," she called. She said this over and over. "Just let go, little mergirl."

Meggie Marie laughed again, then grabbed the bowl and, with both of her hands, spun it hard, then ducked beneath the waves. It felt like a mean spin, not a gentle spin. Like it was meant to scare her. Above Keeper's head, the stars made a dizzy circle. She looked down and the water rushed up. It filled her tiny spinning boat. She was soaking wet and cold and alone. The campfire grew smaller and smaller.

At last Meggie Marie slipped up beside her again and gave the boat a push toward the beach. "Ride the wave ponies!" she shouted again. The boat rocked. The waves galloped beneath it and over it, filling it up. Keeper tried to scream, but her throat was too scared to utter a sound. She was surrounded by waves, their foamy manes curling all around her.

The next thing she knew, Signe was there, yanking her out of the round boat. Signe had found her! She pulled Keeper into her arms. The wave ponies crashed into the sand. At last, the sob rushed out of Keeper, her chest and stomach ached from it. And Signe was shaking. She was holding her and shaking while the waves bumped against them. Signe was furious. There was nothing like Signe's fury, except maybe lightning, hot and sizzling. "Don't ever do that again!" she shouted.

Keeper nodded, up and down. It was a solemn promise that she made when she was three. A promise about going out in the waves.

Then laughter surrounded them, silky and sharp at the same time.

Meggie Marie swam right up next to them. "Signe, you're so serious," she said, swirling the water with her arms, making circles with her fingers. "We were just playing, weren't we, little mergirl?" Then she flipped her long fingers so that the water splashed into their faces; she laughed again. Signe braced herself against the shifting waves.

"What were you thinking?!" Signe shouted at Meggie Marie. Keeper felt the charge course through Signe's arms. Furious.

Then Signe took a step toward Meggie Marie, whose face was silver in the moon's pearled light. There was no shouting now. Instead, Signe looked directly at Meggie Marie's face and said: "You need to go now."

Meggie Marie's face was not laughing now. Instead, there was a different look, a new look. Then she began to shout out the girl's new name, a name she'd never heard before. Not "mergirl" or "Good'un" or "Sweet Pea." No, her new name, "Keeper." Meggie Marie said it over and over.

"Keeper" was in Keeper's ear and throat and chest. "Keeper." It rang around her, in a circle around her head, growing thinner and thinner, until at last there was only

a whisper. Signe turned around and carried Keeper out of the salty sea, carried her to the shore, back to the smoldering campfire. There she pulled the wet T-shirt and bathing suit bottom off of her and wrapped her in the new towel with the blue and red fishes.

Keeper had listened again for her new name, but she couldn't hear anything except the sound of the waves brushing against the sand. How did they get so small?

She looked out toward the dark water and spied a fish's tail, sparkling against the phosphorescent foam of the waves. Then it was gone. The charm around her neck was cold as ice. She started to cry again. She looked at Signe, and Signe was crying too. Signe scooped her up in her towel and tucked her beneath her chin. Together, they cried enough tears to fill up the entire Gulf of Mexico, solid blue.

Now, clinging to the bottom of the boat, Keeper knew.

There was no mermaid mama.

There never had been.

There had only been Meggie Marie, who had almost let her drown on a star-filled night just like this one, who had told her to ride the wave ponies.

Easy peasy!

Suddenly, a blaze of anger shook Keeper's entire body. She yanked hard at the charm around her neck, snapping the pink ribbon, and threw it as hard as she could into the bow of the boat.

97

Somewhere there is a woman, a tall woman, her black hair pulled back. Maybe she is sitting in a café in a mountain town, sipping bitter coffee and eating a croissant; maybe she is on a train passing across the subcontinent of India, watching the monkeys along the tracks scoop up bits of mango that the passengers have tossed to them; maybe she is crossing a street in a large city, some city like New York or Hong Kong or Sydney.

Maybe she thinks about the oyster shell road and her grandmother's house. She has paid the taxes on it every year, right on time. Maybe she will go back there someday.

And maybe, when she thinks about it, she stops what she is doing for just a small moment, looks up and sees the winsome moon. Maybe she thinks about the little daughter she left behind. Maybe.

And maybe she reaches for her heart with her right hand and feels it beating there, remembering that daughter. And maybe she whispers a prayer to the moon, as so many have done before, a prayer to keep watch.

"Keep her," she whispers, "keep her."

98

And Keeper knew this true thing: Signe had kept her.

99

As she hung in the sky, the moon held on to all those prayers from all those mothers, including the newest ones. The moon is the receiver of prayers and songs and even curses. But can the moon answer a prayer? Can she grant a wish?

There are only two things the moon can do for certain. One is to shine her silver light as hard as she can. And the other is to push and pull the tides.

All night long the moon has waited for the stingrays to give her the signal. They had been congregating for days, waiting for this moment. The moon had already pushed the tide up and down once tonight. Such is the way of a summer moon, a blue moon. Now, it is time to raise the tide again. The moon knows this. And so do the stingrays. There were thousands of them gathered up behind the sandbar, just waiting for her to push the tide as high as possible so that they could ride on its back, through the channel and into the Cut. Their bellies are full of the eggs they will lay once there, their mermaids' purses.

They've come for miles for just this occasion. They're waiting, waiting for the moon to give the tide a push.

100

Dogie ran after Too as he headed toward the salty pond. When he got there, he cast the beam from his flashlight along the banks and out onto the water. The water was still low, but he knew that soon it would rush back through the channel and fill it up. He stood there not knowing exactly what he was supposed to see. He had the distinct feeling that something was missing, but what?

"Yep, yep, yep." Too raced onto the pier.

Dogie shone his light toward him. The little dog was pacing back and forth. Then he stopped, right at the end of it.

Where *The Scamper* should be tied, there was nothing. The boat was gone. He scratched his head. He remembered tying a good, strong hitch in the rope.

Could it have come undone? He looked out across the water. It was quiet.

No. He didn't think that the knot could have come undone all by itself on such a calm night. Then another possibility crept into his thoughts: Someone must have taken the boat out.

But who? Who would have taken the boat at this time of night? Mr. Beauchamp? Surely not.

Signe? She had never even been *in* the boat, much less at night.

He cast the flashlight beam out onto the water again. Maybe it had come loose by itself after all. He scanned the light all along the edges of the salt grass marsh. No boat. If it had come loose on the high tide, it would have wedged itself into the swamp grass.

Once again he scanned the marsh. There was no sign of *The Scamper*.

Suddenly, Dogie felt the hair on his arms stand up.

"Oh no," Dogie said.

"Yep, yep, yep," signaled Too.

"Oh no, oh no, oh no," Dogie repeated.

Keeper.

Only Keeper could be out in the boat.

He spun on his heels and rushed across the yard. He bounded up the stairs of the haint blue house and pounded on the door. "Signe!" he shouted. "Signe, wake up!" He turned the knob. It was open.

Keeper had left the door unlocked.

He pushed it open. BD should have been right there, greeting him.

No BD.

Then he realized. *They're out there together.*

"Signe," he shouted again. "Wake up!"

1Ø1

The back of Keeper's neck burnt from where the ribbon had snapped against it. She rolled her head back to lessen the sting. As she leaned back, she noticed that the moon was falling lower in the sky. Then she realized that the water was calming. Bit by bit, the boat settled down until it shuddered like it was catching its breath. Keeper felt like she was being rocked, rocked in a cradle, a small wooden cradle.

Done and undone, dizzy and cold, she stayed curled in the bottom of the boat. Water pooled around her. She wedged her feet tighter against the bench and rested her head on her arms. She could feel the need for sleep travel up her body. She was so, so sleepy. She could fall asleep in an instant. She blinked her eyes. She was too tired to even cry anymore.

She pushed against sleep.

She had to stay awake in case she spotted BD. What if he swam up to her and she didn't see him?

BD.

Her chest ached. The sea grew calmer and calmer. She had lost BD. Every cell felt dislodged, every muscle burnt. Her fingers were cramped from holding on to the bench for such a long time. Her knees were scraped raw.

BD.

The water tapped out his name as it hit the sides of the boat in a steady rhythm: *BD. BD. BD.*

The waves calmed a little more. Her eyes grew heavier and heavier. She sat up. She couldn't let herself fall asleep.

Couldn't let herself . . .

Right then, out of the blue, she heard, "C'mon, c'mon!" Captain! She tensed in preparation for his landing. Sure enough, he crashed into the bottom of the boat just beside her. "C'mon, c'mon," he said. She knew that he was looking for BD. "C'mon, c'mon," he repeated.

"I'm sorry, I'm so, so sorry" was all she could say.

As if the bird understood, he leaned against her chest.

1Ø2

After a while Captain grew weary of leaning. Where was BD? When he had left earlier, the dog was right here in the boat with the girl. Where had he gone? Captain hopped up onto the boat's prow, the highest point. He scanned the entire boat from fore to aft.

No BD. He hopped down and looked underneath the front bench. Was the dog hiding underneath there?

Nope.

No dog.

Then Captain hopped down the middle of the boat and tried to look behind Keeper, where she was wedged against the back bench. Was BD behind her?

"C'mon, c'mon," he called.

Keeper lifted her hand to pat him, but just as her hand came in his direction, he saw, from the corner of his eye, right by the toe of her sneaker . . . shazaam! His fallen star!

His one and only, most magnificent, most highly prized possession of all time, more beautiful and shiny than ever, glimmering in the moonlight. Right there by Keeper's toe. He hopped over to it and plucked it right up. *Brrrr . . .* it was just as cold as he remembered it.

But cold schmold, it didn't matter. It was his fallen star. He had found it again, calloo callay!

And because how valuable is a prize if you can't show it off, he carried it right to Keeper and stood directly in front of her face. He could not say his customary "c'mon, c'mon" without dropping the charm, so he did the only other thing he could think of. He tapped her cheek with it.

1Ø3

The cold of the charm against her face gave Keeper a start. She blinked her eyes and looked right at the golden disk. Her lucky charm. It was still strung on the snapped pink ribbon.

"Ha!" she said to Captain. "Some lucky charm."

Still, she was glad that the bird was with her. If only she had a chunk of watermelon to give him.

Watermelon!

That was it! Keeper pushed herself up to a sitting position.

The charm. Watermelon. The charm. Watermelon.

With her fingers shaking from the cold, she tried to pry the charm out of Captain's beak. She gave it a tug, but there was no getting the charm away from him. Her hands were so sore, she couldn't get a good grip.

Only one thing to do . . .

"Watermelon," she said as loud as she could with her raspy voice.

"C'mon, c'mon!" he cried. And with that, he dropped the charm right into her hand. As quickly as she could manage with her fumbling fingers, she looped the ribbon around Captain's neck and tied it.

Then she rasped, "Watermelon, Captain. Go find watermelon."

Captain knew exactly what she meant. And he also knew exactly where to find it. At the haint blue house. Keeper didn't have to ask him twice. Just the mention of watermelon, and he was there. To help him launch, she lifted him into the air with both hands and watched as he flew up up up and then disappeared.

"Maybe," she said to the sky, "maybe . . . maybe . . . maybe . . . maybe . . . ," until, exhausted, Keeper leaned back against the bench and closed her eyes. Sleep pulled her under its welcoming sheets.

She did not see the fin break the surface of the water. She did not see the moon slide down toward the horizon.

104

How far can a land dog swim?

As soon as BD fell into the water, he tried to get back to the boat, back to Keeper. He paddled his front legs as hard as he could, but just as he was about to reach the boat, a huge wave separated them. He paddled and paddled and paddled until his whole body burnt. The life vest helped keep him on the top of the water, but it was also popping up under his chin, making it even more difficult for him to catch his breath.

His lungs felt like they were on fire. He couldn't see anything but water. He couldn't see the boat, couldn't see his girl, couldn't see the moon.

But even though every muscle cried out in pain, he kept swimming until he couldn't swim anymore.

Finally, he stopped and let himself be carried.

Carried by the water.

Carried by the waves.

Carried by two strong arms, all the way to the shore, where he lay down on the edge of the surf and let himself be carried into darkness.

If someone else were watching, maybe a shrimp boat sailor or treasure hunter, they might have cried, "Monster!" But that is not what BD saw at all. Only an old swimmer with hair as white as snow and eyes the color of the sky. Where his legs should be, a fish's tail. And down his back, a fin.

1Ø5

The dog was not the first one Jacques de Mer had carried to this strip of beach along the Texas coast.

The first was the drowned body of a little boy, so quiet in the deep waters. He had found him just past the sandbar that jutted up out of the waves.

When he looked at the boy's silent face, he knew that someone was missing him. Didn't he know about missing? He recognized missing when he saw it, even on the face of the drowned boy, so he had tenderly lifted the small body and carried it to shore.

But that had been a mistake. A shrimper had caught sight of him and called out, called out to his comrades, "Monster! The monster has taken the child and drowned him!"

He had swum away as quickly as he could to avoid

the cruel nets and dangerous rifles of the others. More than that, he had swum away from that word, "monster." The cruelest word in the world.

He had not returned to these waters for years and years. He thought he would never come back here. Ever.

But then tonight, out of the blue, he had gotten a signal, a signal to swim back here, to this lonely patch of coastline, along the Texas coast. He should have known that it could not have been the same signal he had been waiting for all these years.

It had taken all of his courage to carry the dog onto the shore. What if another fisherman saw him again? What then? Would they hunt him down? He had only barely escaped last time.

And the dog was so spent. He wasn't even sure if he would make it. Nevertheless, he could tell that the dog was important to that little girl.

And now, what about her?

All alone in the small boat?

What was she doing out there? He swam back to

the red boat, leaned over the side, and saw her sleeping. This was a child who was loved; it was obvious on her face that she had been well taken care of. A beloved child. Friend to a beloved dog. He had seen her sorrow when the dog slipped over the edge.

So as quietly as he could, he swam behind *The Scamper* and pushed it toward the distant shore.

He looked up at the sky. The sun would rise soon. He couldn't risk swimming all the way in again, so instead, he let out a low whistle. In an instant the stingrays—water angels—surrounded the boat. Hundreds of them. Thousands. A flotilla of stingrays.

"Take her," he told them. "Keep her with you until you reach the sandbar," and as he watched, he saw the beautiful rays, their wings wide and gentle, steer the little boat toward the shore and lodge it against De Vaca's Rock.

And then he swam away.

1Ø6

Signe's entire body hummed with worry. She was crazy with it. Electrified by it, as if she might throw off sparks if she touched anything. How could she have let this happen?

This was all her fault. If she had not yelled at Keeper about the talking crabs and mermaids, her girl would still be sleeping in the room next to hers, right where she was supposed to be.

She needed to call someone, but who? Dogie handed her the phone.

She called them all: the Coast Guard, the sheriff, the police. She even called the veterinarian, Dr. Scarmardo, the only veterinarian in Tater. Woke him up and then didn't know what to say.

And all of them told her to wait by the phone.

Coast Guard: "Please wait by the phone, ma'am."

Sheriff: "We'll be right there, please wait by the phone."

Police: "Stay by your phone."

Dr. Scarmardo: "I'll be there in an hour."

They all said: Wait by the phone.

"How?" she had screamed. How could she wait by the phone, wait for an hour, when Keeper was out at sea in a boat that was meant for a pond? ALL BY HERSELF!!! Signe felt like her skin was pulling away from her bones, like she would fly apart any second, like the world was coming undone, unwound, unglued. She felt like she needed to run into the water herself, to swim from one end of the gulf to the next.

"That's it," she said.

She would not wait by the phone. She couldn't.

And like a bolt of lightning, Signe was on the move. She flew out the door and ran down the steps.

And Dogie ran beside her, followed by Too.

They ran, all the way to the beach, and then stopped right at the water's edge. Suddenly, the enormity of the gulf, so dark and restless, overcame Signe. All she knew for certain was that Keeper was out there. Somewhere. And then, beside her, Dogie lifted his voice and called . . .

107

"KEEEEEPPPPPEEEEERRRRR!!!!!

1Ø8

"KEEEEEPPPPPEEEEERRRRR!!!!!

109

"KEEEEEPPPPPEEEEERRRRR!!!!!"

110

Surely, Signe thought, Keeper couldn't have gone far, could she?

How far could a little girl in a boat go?

Could *The Scamper* manage in the deep water beyond the breakers?

Signe put her hands against her cheeks; she rubbed her eyes with her fingertips.

More and more questions flew into her head. Tears, a million of them, a trillion of them, blazed down her face.

She should have told Keeper long ago, told her about her mother, told her that she, Signe, had made her leave, told her that Meggie Marie was no mermaid. But instead, she had let Keeper believe in things like elves and tooth fairies and crabs that talked.

Oh, what had she done? What had she *not* done? And then the cruelest question of all: What kind of mother was she?

On the water's edge, her feet sinking clear to the middle of the earth, Signe's knees buckled and she slumped down into the wet sand.

"Keep her," she whimpered, "I was supposed to keep her."

Signe looked out again across the rolling breakers, so many of them, so tall, the phosphorescent foam glittering in the dark. She felt Dogie standing beside her, and suddenly, a sound that she had never heard before slipped from her body, a low wail that wrapped itself around her chest and her hips and her knees until it felt like it would suffocate her right there in the sand.

Signe tried to stop, tried to make the sound end, but she couldn't.

She closed her eyes. If she stayed here, as tight as an oyster in a shell, packed into the sand, would the sea come and get her? She didn't think she could ever move from this spot, from this position. She didn't think she could ever stop the hideous sound that wouldn't stop couldn't stop wouldn't stop couldn't—

Just then Dogie wrapped his arms around her shoulders and gently pulled her up. Then he lifted her into his broad arms and just held her, held her while the sound just kept sliding from the deepest part of her throat and belly and feet, her whole body. He stood there at the edge of the entire world and held on to her, the most tender holding in the universe, until finally, the sound was done with her and flew away.

"Let's just wait," he said. She could only nod. She had no other sound left in her, none at all. And in the meantime, the tide had come closer and closer and closer while the sky got lighter and lighter and lighter.

111

Yemaya.

She doesn't grant just any wish. She is old. She is cranky. She is hard of hearing.

But her heart is not as crusty as some may think. As one by one the small figures found their way through the waters, she began to smile. Gifts.

She lined them up on her undersea dresser in a parade and admired the artistry. There was Sedna and Lorelei, the siren, the *ningyo*, and the *rusalka* and the *Meerfrau*. The *rusalka*, with her tangled hair, made her laugh. She tossed it above her head and caught it again.

Yemaya, she just loves to laugh. It fills her round belly with happy. Makes her think, *Just one wish.*

The girl called out for her mother. Yes? Not a hard wish at all.

Yemaya.

She will grant that wish.

112

Just as Signe began to believe that Dogie might have to hold her until the end of time, there on the water's edge she heard a familiar sound.

"C'mon, c'mon!"

Dogie stepped aside. Captain landed with a thud at their feet. "C'mon, c'mon," he cried.

It was not completely light yet, but Signe could see an odd gleam coming from the bird's neck. She reached down, but the bird hopped to one side. "C'mon, c'mon," he urged again.

Signe reached for him, and before he could get away again, she caught him. She held him with both hands firmly on his wings to keep him from flapping. Then she tucked him beneath her arm and looked.

"The charm!" she cried.

She recognized it, the charm that Meggie Marie had given Keeper right before she left. Meggie Marie had told her that a seagull had dropped it in her hand. Signe hadn't believed it. But here it was, tied around Captain's neck. And there was the pink ribbon, the one she had given to Keeper just because.

Then she knew. It was a message. Keeper had tied the charm around Captain's neck. It was a message from Keeper. *Hurry*, it said. *Hurry.*

113

In her sleep Keeper felt the bump when the little boat hit the sandbar. She opened her eyes. The sky was still dark, but the moon cast enough light for her to see. She sat up and looked over the sides of the boat. Sand.

Sand!

And the rock! De Vaca's Rock!

The tide must have pushed her back this way.

In front of her, she could see the shadows of home. Home! She was almost there. Suddenly, she had to get there. Everything in her, every bone, every sinew, every cell called for home.

"Signe," she croaked. Her voice was just a whisper, but it didn't matter. She just needed to get to Signe, to home.

She scrambled over the edge of the boat and

stepped onto the jutting sandbar. It was harder than she thought it would be, not sandy at all, but rocky. Solid.

Her legs were wobbly. Her whole body was wobbly. She squatted down beside the boat and held on to it to try to steady herself. The tide, she could tell, had turned back around and was spilling onto the beach a hundred yards in front of her. Only a hundred yards. Could she make it?

A thin pink line of light slipped over the horizon.

Pink. Like her ribbon. She reached up to touch the charm, then remembered that she had given it to Captain. Had the seagull made his way back? Would Signe know what it meant?

And then, as if in answer to her question, she heard her name. "Keeper! Keeper!" Only this time it wasn't coming from the waves. It wasn't a whisper. It wasn't a memory. It didn't come from a mermaid or a haint.

Just like electricity, an enormous jolt of happiness charged through her, from the tips of her toes to the top of her head. *Zing!*

"Keeper! Keeper!"

Her name again!

It was Signe.

Calling her.

Signe!

She looked toward the beach. And there was Signe, wading into the water just as she had seven long years ago, standing in the surf up to her knees, calling her.

"I'm coming," Keeper tried to shout, but her voice was completely gone. It didn't matter. She pulled her life vest as tightly around herself as she could and jumped right into the shallow water. Keeper hurried and hurried; she swam just like she had seen all those surfers do every day of her life, just as she had learned in the Tater Municipal Swimming Pool. She pushed herself through the water, she rode the waves, rode right on their backs, rode them straight into the arms of Signe.

114

As soon as they got to the beach, Dogie picked Keeper up. He slung her onto his broad back, just like he had when she was small. She pressed her face into his ropy dreadlocks. They were scratchy, but she didn't care. She held on to him. Beside them, Signe held on to her too.

Here in this small corner of the world unto itself, they all held on. A family.

115

The problem was, there was a family member missing. BD.

All the happiness that Keeper had felt when Signe swam out to her evaporated in the missing of BD.

"BD," she tried to say, but her throat was too raw for words. She mouthed his name again and again, tears streaming down her face, but all that came out was a rasp.

As Keeper clung to Dogie, the loss of BD grew and grew, until it felt as huge as a mountain. Huger.

Keeper reached for Signe.

"We'll look for him, Sweet Pea" was all that Signe could say.

And Keeper sobbed.

116

Meanwhile, as much as Keeper loved BD, someone else loved him too. Does it seem odd that a seagull and a dog would be such friends? Perhaps. But ever since that stormy night when that nasty winter wind blew Captain through the kitchen window, when BD had wrapped his warm body around the seagull to keep him from shivering in pain and fright, Captain had adored that dog.

Now he circled the dog lying on the beach, there on the water's edge, flew right down beside him and nestled up, right under his chin.

"C'mon, c'mon," he whispered. But the dog didn't move.

Captain hopped right up on BD's side. The dog was

so still. Captain stared at him for a very long time. He walked in a circle all around his best friend. Then he walked in the other direction. Only one thing to do. He flapped his wings and shot into the air.

In minutes he circled the group on the beach— Keeper, Dogie, Signe, and Too—flew right up into their faces.

"C'mon, c'mon," he cried.

And for the second time that day, he delivered a message.

117

The world is full of mystery, isn't it?

How do the stingrays know when to migrate to the sandbar in time for the moon to light their way into the Cut and then back out again?

When does a star decide it's done with burning and fall to the earth?

Why do the manatees swim with mermaids?

How does a good dog know that his girl needs him as much as he needs her?

Questions for the universe.

And here's another question: How can that same good dog deliver up so many stealth kisses at one time? When Keeper finally found BD, right at the water's edge, life vest still intact, he washed her face in one stealth kiss after another. Keeper found her finder dog.

118

It seems like the story might end there, but when so many wishes had been cast about in a single night, at least a few of them have to come true. Yemaya, after all, is not the only one who can grant a wish. Let's not forget that the moon has a part to play when it comes to matters of love.

Sure enough, while they all walked along the beach, the familiar tune of the two-word song entered Dogie's head and wouldn't let go. Suddenly, he began to hum it, even without his ukulele. And before he knew what he was doing, Dogie reached over and took Signe's hand. Then, right there in front of everyone, he knelt down beside her on one knee and said those two words. He said them without a single stutter. Clear as a bell. Said them right to Signe: "Marry me."

Signe looked at him, surprised.

Then Dogie said them again, even more clearly this time: "Marry me."

Signe was silent. She had waited for this moment for such a long time. Ten years. Ever since the day she had first seen him, the day Keeper was born.

A tear ran down her cheek, and when she rubbed it away with her palm, she actually blushed, something she had not done in years. Then, just like in the movies, just like in old fairy tales, Dogie pulled her toward him and kissed her.

Just like that.

And Signe?

She said yes!

119

Several days later Keeper sat at the kitchen table. Signe sat next to her, filling out all the reports left by the sheriff and the Coast Guard and even Dr. Scarmardo, the veterinarian, who had proclaimed BD as fit as a fiddle.

Where the wooden bowl used to rest on the counter, there was a pot of replanted antique roses. She and Signe had gone over to Mr. Beauchamp's house and helped him repot his roses and night-blooming cyrus, and he had insisted that they bring some of the roses home with them. Now they sat on the table, bright pink, like Keeper's ribbon.

Mr. Beauchamp had been glad to see them, but Keeper noticed that he looked older than ever.

"Barnacles," he told them. "I'm as old as barnacles."

But this time he did not chuckle when he said it. He did not add "*mon petite.*" Instead, he stayed in his rocking chair and rubbed Sinbad's black-and-white fur and gazed out over the water.

Now Keeper sat at the kitchen table with her red purse, counting her money. She had $44.00. As soon as her hands had felt better, she'd resumed her duties as official waxwing. In front of her, she had the Sears catalogue that Signe had brought home, the "Wish Book" edition. Signe had told her to save it for a rainy day.

But Keeper had a better idea. Why spend money on a rainy day when she could spend it on a happy day? Keeper had dog-eared the exact page. She had found the perfect wedding gift for Dogie and Signe—a new, stainless-steel cooking pot. Exactly. The price was $34.95, which meant that once she added tax and shipping, she would probably have just the right amount, with maybe a little extra for gift wrapping.

When she showed the photo to Signe, Signe smiled and said, "Sausage gumbo. No more crabs."

But as Keeper looked at the roses on the table, she felt regret. Once she paid for the new gumbo pot, she would not have enough left over to repay Mr. Beauchamp for his broken pots, especially those for his night-blooming cyrus.

Even if she waxed surfboards every day for hours, it would take her months, maybe years, to repay Mr. Beauchamp for his losses. She rested her elbows on the table and held her face in her hands.

The only thing of any value that she owned was the charm.

That was it! Her mother's charm.

Keeper had no need for it now, that was for sure. She scooped it out of her dresser drawer again, still icy cold, and put it in her pocket.

"Cooleoleo!" she said, then she walked out the door, down the steps, and across the road to Mr. Beauchamp's house.

That very night Henri Beauchamp stood by the water and held the charm in his hand. It was warm, like it was all those years ago in that village by the sea on the southern coast of France. He held it over his heart and made a wish. Sinbad curled up at his feet and purred.

A short time later, sitting on his porch in the darkness, he swore he heard the soft nicker of a charcoal gray mare. Or maybe it was just the wind.

And just off the coast, not too far away, in a deep puddle of moonbeams, the old swimmer raised his head above the water. There it was again, the old *porte-bonheur*, only this time the message was unmistakable. At last, he knew, the charm was in the right hands. Jack ducked beneath the water and swam as fast as he could.

12,0

Dogie and Signe said their vows right there on the beach, with Keeper and BD and Too and even Sinbad all there as witnesses.

Even Dogie's mother was there, arrived all the way from New Jersey along with his great-uncle Sylvester. "I have to meet my new granddaughter, don't I?" Dogie's mother said. And straightaway, she started in on hugging. She hugged Keeper, she hugged Dogie and Signe, she even hugged BD and Too. It was hug city.

And there were also two old men, sitting in lawn chairs. In the shirt pocket of one was the long-lost *porte-bonheur*; he could feel the warmth of it through the fabric of his shirt.

In the lawn chair next to him, just as old and

wrinkled as he, sat Jack, his eyes as blue as the sky. They held hands, like they did so long ago.

And Keeper?

Beside her stands BD, finder of missing sandals and wooden spoons and Popsicle sticks. Captain is perched on his broad back like a jockey astride a horse. With one hand, Keeper pats BD's soft head. In her other, she holds a carving of an old woman. Somehow, it remained safe in Keeper's pocket. She's the only one of the original seven merlings left. Keeper curls her fingers around it and holds it against her heart. She had asked for a wish. A wish for her mother to find her, and she had.

"Yemaya," she whispers, "thank you." And she tucks the tiny carving into her pocket. There it nestles beside her new merling, the one just finished, of Jacques de Mer. Mr. Beauchamp carved it out of the old piece of juniper that Keeper had found on the beach. Juniper, a tree that grows in the Camargue region of France.

Keeper looks out at the blue-green Gulf of Mexico, the sun turning the waves to silver. She takes a small paper boat from her back pocket, dubbed "The Perfect Plan," straightens its folds, and sets it atop the water where she thinks it might sail to the sandbar.

Legend has it that it might have been a mermaid who lured Cabeza de Vaca onto that rock five hundred years ago. It could have been.

In the shallows of the Cut, a manatee raises its head above the water, then dips back under and disappears.

Author's Note

My Texas town of Tater is completely fictional, as is the world unto itself known as Oyster Ridge Road. However, the Spanish explorer Álva Núñez Cabeza de Vaca did run aground in 1528 near Galveston Island, known at that time as the Isle of Misfortune, probably because of the vicious storms that pummeled it from time to time. Once ashore, Cabeza de Vaca spent several years with the coastal tribe known as the Karankawa, or the Clamcoehs, first as a slave and later as a respected member of their community.

Some of the only written accounts that we have of this coastal band, as well as several others, are from Cabeza de Vaca's journal, *La Relación*, which is available in its entirety online at: http://alkek.library.tx state.edu/swwc/cdv. It's important to remember that Cabeza de Vaca's view is that of a European, but the journal is nevertheless a detailed documentation of sixteenth-century Texas and its inhabitants.

Useful information can also be found through the

Texas State History Museum at: tshaonline.org/handbook/online/articles/KK/bmk5.html.

The ponies of the Camargue are among the world's last surviving wild horses. Over the centuries they have adapted to life in the swampy regions of the Rhone Delta of southern France. There was a lovely film made in 1953 by Albert Lamorisse called *Crin Blanc*, or *White Mane*, which is about a boy who tames a Camargue stallion. When I think about my character Henri Beauchamp, I imagine that when he was fifteen, he was something like the young hero Folco of Lamorisse's movie. For more information go to: janusfilms.com/redandwhite.

Sandbars have a lot of names: shoals, gravebars, even spits. They are typically created by wave action and are made up of a combination of granular material, including sand, pebbles, and rocks. Many come and go, depending upon the direction and volume of the waves. But some build up over time and become barrier islands.

The first time I ever stepped on a sandbar off the

beach of Galveston, I was surprised by its solidity. It wasn't so much sand as sandstone. Older sandbars can begin as reefs, such as one made by an oyster bed, which give them a certain amount of rigidity and longevity. I imagine that my fictional sandbar is in this latter group and that it could easily be thought of as a rock. Thus, De Vaca's Rock.

Other things have names too. For example, crabs technically have pincers. But I have taken liberties with the word and called them "pinchers," which is the way my ear always heard them when I was growing up, and after all, that's what they do—*pinch*.

Surfers definitely have their own language. When my sisters and I were teenagers, we owned a surfboard called a "gun." It's a flat-out miracle that we didn't hurt ourselves in our attempts to gun for a big wave. And while I've never personally heard a surfer say "cooleoleo," legend has it that it was, indeed, surfers who first coined the term. I vote for bringing that delicious word into the regular lexicon.

As for the mer, find a body of water. . . .

Acknowledgments

Here's a true thing: A teller can spin a tale only if there are people around the campfire to help her keep that story from spinning away. I am indebted to Kimberly Willis Holt, Jeanette Ingold, Lola Schaefer, and Rebecca Kai Dotlich, who read the earliest messy draft and stopped short of telling me to toss it back to the sharks. Candace Leslie listened when I needed a listener, and so did Rose Eder and Janet Jones.

I am particularly grateful for the care offered up by Randall Brown, Debbie Leland, and Uma Krishnaswami, each of whom encouraged me to rewrite the ending. Maybe the dude on the beach will find his own story, eh?

As always, a boatload of gratitude goes to Dennis Foley. He's my anchorman.

When I felt like I might drown, Diane Linn threw a rope and helped bring the whole story into sharper focus. She lovingly cast her knowledge of tides and currents and stingrays my way, and she asked me to consider heartbreak over anger. Thank you!

And always, always, my brilliant editor, Caitlyn Dlouhy, believed in the magic of Keeper's tale, even when my own doubts felt overwhelming. She helped me find my Keeper—yep, she did. Assistant editor Kiley Frank kept the oars in the water throughout the long process. A writer needs navigation, especially in rough waters, and that's what Jeannie Ng provided. As well, my agents, Emily E. vanBeek and Holly McGhee, and my kindred Pips, kept the light burning, a beacon.

Right along on the edge of the water, my late grandmother Marge, my personal haint, walks between the pages of this book. She lived in Galveston, where I spent many happy hours and days as a child. It was her very real BD and Captain and green Dodge station wagon, her house by the marsh where the stingrays laid their mermaids' purses, with its wrap-around porch, that offered up this story. Marge always called me a "keeper." It's what I wish for every child, to feel that way, completely loved and cherished. I know she would have swum through the sea at night to find me.

In my world unto itself, I am blessed to have many people who keep watch. I am a better person and a better writer because of my colleagues and students at Vermont College of Fine Arts. I'm a nicer person because of my mom, Patricia Childress, who continues to steer the craft; Laini Bostian, who sends me mermaids in the mail; my two sons, Jacob and Cooper, who are my true heart; and my sweet and handsome Ken, whom I love like crazy and always will.